Derek waved his men back and slipped the hatchet from his belt. Keeping to the low-lying ground where the fog was thickest, he crept silently forward. The last thing that the Brotherhood of Diablo expected was for the vermin they had penned up here to attack them. Nonetheless, the guard did wear a helmet, which meant Margo's cold-blooded technique was perhaps the only way he could be killed in silence.

Derek waited until the guard was a few steps past him, then sprang silently out of the fog, sweeping his hatchet in a low plane. It severed the guard's spinal column at the base of his back, killing him instantly. Derek braced himself to catch the huge trunk as it folded over the lower half of its body, so that no heavy clattering fall would attract attention.

Willie was at his side before he had even wrestled the dead weight to the ground. He whispered anxiously, "One of the Mogs woke up a couple of minutes ago and left the encampment area."

Derek hesitated; this was something completely unexpected

"We can't g

last. "They'd o

the next day. Le

Look for these other TOR books by Jack Lovejoy

MAGUS REX
A VISION OF BEASTS: CREATION DESCENDING
A VISION OF BEASTS: THE SECOND KINGDOM

A TOM DOHERTY ASSOCIATES BOOK

A VISION OF BEASTS: THE BROTHERHOOD OF DIABLO

First printing: May 1985

A TOR Book

Published by Tom Doherty Associates
8-10 West 36 Street
New York, N.Y. 10018

Cover art by Victoria Poyser

ISBN: 0-812-54504-4
CAN. ED.: 0-812-54505-2

Printed in the United States of America

CONTENTS

Chapter 1: The Buried City

On the benches of every galley, in every underground slave pen, among all who wore chains on the fortress island of Diablo, the name Derek the Hunter had come to be venerated; not as evidence that such a person really existed, but only as a symbol, a shimmering hope of deliverance, a legendary hero. Now, the legend had suddenly revived, brighter and more vivid than ever—although many still believed that the man now calling himself Derek the Hunter was only a slave like themselves, who had somehow escaped and adopted the name as a rallying cry, or a last doomed gesture. Such things had happened before.

Few slaves on Diablo reached any advanced age, but it was repeated to this day that many years ago a revolt had actually succeeded in killing some Rathugs before being mercilessly crushed. It was also repeated, in whispers, that it had taken the wretched survivors days, even weeks, to die; that when the torturers had at last finished with them, their poor broken bodies, some still alive, were hardly fit to be thrown to the dog-things. Their cries of agony seemed to echo down the years, reminding all the world of the fate in store for any who would oppose the Brotherhood of Diablo.

And yet the legend of Derek the Hunter continued to grow stronger, despite the certainty of being condemned to the pits beneath the Rath of Diablo for even mentioning the name. Nor were the horrors awaiting there mere legend.

It was even suspected that there was now more than one escaped slave using the name. The sudden forays seemed to erupt everywhere at once, then nowhere, like the lambent flickering of a candle that never quite goes out. Although few slaves had been liberated thus far, and no outwork seriously ravaged, the Invincibles seemed for once powerless to avenge themselves.

The entire island of Diablo was one vast network of strongholds whose every garrison and patrol was ultimately concentrated upon the Rath of Diablo itself. But these defenses were all turned inward; raised not as bulwarks to keep enemies out—who would dare attack the invincible Brotherhood of Diablo?—but as an enclosure to keep their own slaves in. They were ineffective thus far against a handful of rebels who somehow anticipated every move against them.

"The Rathugs never stay down here at night," said Willie, keeping his voice low. "But you always have to watch out for their spies and Judases. There's always a few of them around, no matter where you go."

Exactly how the city had been buried, Derek could only guess. He remembered reading in a book called *The Last Days of Pompeii* how an ancient Roman city was buried beneath volcanic ash. Old Tom, who had lived in these parts as a boy, had recounted to him that volcanic eruptions had indeed been triggered by the cataclysm, eruptions which had spewed countless tons of ash and lava all along the contorting and buckling coastline, and that these in turn had triggered cloudbursts of torrential rain. Perhaps the volcanic ashes had thus been liquified into a deadly batter which inundated the city? However it happened, the city was not buried in ashes but in a substance now almost as hard as rock. Those condemned to mine it were the most wretched of all the driven and brutalized hordes of slaves on Diablo.

"If they're left alone down here at night," Derek whispered, as they crept down the deserted shaft, "Why don't they tunnel their way out and escape?"

"I was hoping you wouldn't ask me that," sighed Willie. "But it wasn't my fault. They used to stick pins into me, and keep me awake for hours and hours until I thought I was going to die. I couldn't help it, Derek.''

He had to stop and comfort the affectionate little creature, who looked close to tears, before he could get him to continue.

''They used to carry me in a wooden cage up and down the hills above the city, but I would always say that I couldn't find anybody trying to dig his way out. Then one day they tricked me. They had some of their spies and Judases dig a test shaft. I knew they were there, of course, but when I pretended . . .'' He shuddered. ''After that I could never tell if the slaves were really trying to dig their way out, or if it was just another trick. Anyway, there were usually a few Mogs patrolling the hills at night, and you know yourself that the Rathugs always let them have anybody they catch trying to escape.'' He shuddered again.

''Are they roving the hills tonight?''

''More than ever—since they haven't got me anymore.'' His nature was as happy and resilient as Jana's, and he laughed merrily at the thought.

But Derek had never felt as depressed as he did tonight. Would he never find a place in the sun? Were all his battles to be fought in squalid tunnels beneath the earth? He had been continually on the run ever since being stranded with Willie and Buck here on Diablo, but had so far accomplished almost nothing. He had watched the morale of the handful of slaves he had liberated decline along with his own.

Without Willie, they would all have been captured a dozen times over by now.

But not even Willie could tell him whether Eva was safe. Over and over again they had watched helplessly as enemy fleets—once he counted over a hundred ships—embarked for the farther shores of the New Sea, toward the haven of his own people. How many had been killed or captured? Was the Wise Woman again working in collusion with the Brotherhood of Diablo? All that Willie could tell him was that Jana was still alive, somewhere to the north.

Nor was there any way of escaping Diablo. There had been a mountain range before the cataclysm, and for much of its rugged coastline sheer walls of rock plunged into the raging sea; even where there was access to the coast, labyrinthine reefs and shoals made navigation even by canoe hazardous at night. During the day, the black hulks of the enemy's galleys could be seen patrolling off shore. He had once spotted a scout ship from the Fisherfolk; but it was so far out at sea that there was no way of signaling it.

Had Eva been trying futilely to contact him? Did she even know that he was still living, that he had not yet been killed or captured? Perhaps all that Jana could tell her in turn was that Willie was still alive, somewhere on Diablo.

"No wonder the Rathugs don't like staying down here at night." Willie looked apprehensively up at the ceiling. "Some of these shafts look ready to fall on our heads."

Other than the asphalt pavement beneath their feet, nothing around them in fact looked very reliable. The shafts here had been dug when the Brotherhood of Diablo first began quarrying the buried city, and such props as there were seemed uncomfortably old and rotted; even the encasing rock was no harder than sun-baked clay. A series of regular branch tunnels, burrowing into what had been a row of shops lining one of the city's main streets, diverged left and right all along the crumbling old shaft. But at least there were no human or non-human creatures to worry about here. Willie had not bothered to lower his voice.

"Can you tell yet how many people are down here?" asked Derek.

Willie stood for a moment with his head bent forward. "About fifty or sixty," he said at last. "That's probably just the regular crew. Whenever they find something valuable—especially machines of any kind—they bring in crews from outside. If it's very valuable, they even bring in the crews from the other buried cities."

"There are five of them in all, you said?"

"Yes, but none as big as this one. They're all in a line facing the sea. . . ." He suddenly fell silent.

Derek tensed, and unconsciously reached for his sword—the same reaction Willie and Jana displayed whenever they sensed approaching danger.

"A Mog," Willie said aloud, pointing directly overhead. "I hope he's not too heavy—I really don't trust that ceiling. It's a shame we couldn't bring Buck with us down here.''

Derek smiled. That was another similarity between Jana and Willie—their dependence on Buck to carry them beyond trouble.

''Don't worry, Buck will be safe where he is.''

''That's not exactly what I meant,'' Willie muttered, again glancing uneasily up at the ceiling.

The section of the quarry they now entered was newer and much more firmly buttressed. The encasing rock was also firmer, and hence that much more arduous to mine; so much more arduous in fact that no mere fifty or sixty men could possibly have cleared such a vast area in so short a time. That meant that special workgangs had been brought in from the outside after some very important discovery. But what? All Derek could see was the base of a multistoried granite building, fronted by large showcase windows, a few miraculously still unbroken.

''That's where all the slaves are.'' Willie now lowered his voice. ''Straight ahead, but above us.''

''And the men are guarded only by these spies and Judases?'' Derek whispered.

''Not really guarded—the spies and Judases work right along with the others—but the slaves know that whatever they say or do will be reported to the Rathugs.''

''Why don't the men make sure that these wretches don't report anything to anybody, ever again?''

''Kill them?'' Willie shook his head. ''In fact,

they always do the hardest and most dangerous jobs for them, because if a spy or Judas is found dead—for whatever reason—every member of his workgang is executed. We'll have to watch out for them ourselves," he whispered. "So they don't sneak up to the surface and squeal on us. The Rathugs would be down here fast enough then!"

"But how can we identify these spies and Judases?"

"Oh, that's easy. They're never chained up for the night like the others."

The lavish use of kerosene lanterns in every shaft of the quarry was one more indication of the lavish supplies of fuel available here on Diablo. The region seemed to have been a major producer of fuel before the cataclysm. Once the Brotherhood of Diablo had their machines operative, they would not lack the means to run them—and would use them until they had subjugated every surviving bastion of freedom still left in the world.

This was just one more reason urging Derek to so dangerous a venture here in the buried city. Freeing men here would give him at least the option of more effective raids and diversions—anything to delay the build-up of the Brotherhood of Diablo into true invincibility. More free men might also permit the liberation of others. Most important of all, it could allow him to exploit any chance opportunity for contacting Eva. The Brotherhood of Diablo was not yet invincible—but only through the coordination of every usable weapon, resource, or pocket of resistance against them could their inexorable build-up even be delayed.

"These ceilings look much stronger," Willie said with relief, lowering his voice to a whisper. "Seems like a strange way to arrange furniture, though."

But Derek had recognized the nature of the building the moment they stepped inside. All along the wandering route from Saluston he had encountered similar structures, although none quite so grand and well-stocked. It was a department store; a treasure house of tools and machines. No wonder the Rathugs had brought in crews from outside to help dig it out. Maybe he could find some tools here himself.

The aisles of furniture, cooking and refrigeration units, and racks of electrical devices were covered with a furry blanket of dust. There were only a few footprints on the floor, as if these aisles had been abandoned after a single cursory inspection. Derek abandoned them as well.

Down one aisle only was there evidence of heavy traffic; very heavy traffic; the tile flooring was well-trampled and scored by ponderous objects being dragged across it toward the entrance. Much of this traffic led from a stairway down to the basement.

Derek glanced questioningly at Willie—who shook his head—then silently lifted one of the kerosene lanterns from the wall, and tiptoed down the stairs. At the top of them stood a sign: HARDWARE, GARDEN EQUIPMENT, LUNCH COUNTER. Had all the tools already been looted?

At the bottom of the stairs was an aisle lined with what Derek recognized as ‘‘garden equipment’’; but the many open spaces indicated that most of the larger samples had already been hauled away, presumably machines of some kind. Beyond this stretched a long counter covered with yellow plastic, strips of shiny metal, and dust; in front of it stretched a row of round stools at the top of shiny metal posts.

Derek made the mistake of brushing against one of these as he passed, and it spun round and round with a soft enticing whirr. As he continued down the aisle, he did not notice that he was now alone.

The hardware section was even now in the process of being looted; most of the counters and wall-racks were already bare, but some of the rough wooden crates into which tools and equipment were being packed still lay open on the floor. Saws, hammers, and chisels would probably be the most useful in cutting through chains, and he found all he needed. What he did not find, when he at last turned around, was Willie.

Silently laying down the tools, he stole swiftly back up the aisle, his heart pounding with apprehension, his hand reaching for his sword. Then he heard the soft enticing whirr again, and there was Willie—spinning giddily round and round on one of the revolving stools in front of the lunch counter, laughing merrily.

Derek now realized that he would have to watch him more closely among so many enticements, especially when they passed through the toy department. He helped him down and waited, until after a few dizzily uncertain steps he at last restabilized. Then they collected the tools from the hardware department.

Returning to the ground floor, Derek found a directory on a pillar beside a small department marked HEALTH FOODS. There turned out to be four storys, and he was happy to see that the toy department was on the topmost.

The narrow stairway to the second floor had strangely grooved metal steps, with loose rubber handrails at either side. At the top was a large block arrow pointing toward BEDROOM FURNISHINGS. Willie indicated that the workgang was sleeping in that same direction.

A lantern in one hand, a canvas bag of tools in the other, Derek strode silently into their midst. He had also taken a coil of rope from the hardware department, and the three men who were not chained down for the night woke up to find themselves being tied down to their canopied four-poster bed. Then he went to work with the tools, but.quickly discovered that the slaves themselves were more adept at their use than he was. Meanwhile he introduced himself.

"I am called Derek the Hunter." All work on the chains ceased at once, and he had to beckon them to continue. "Are your lives here so precious that you won't risk them for the chance of living as free men? For the chance of fighting back against the Brotherhood of Diablo?"

Their reaction was such as to make the three tied-up men look very uncomfortable, despite their luxurious resting place. Their discomfort grew with the clatter of each chain or shackle that dropped to the floor. For there could be no doubt that these were the most brutalized of all the slaves on Diablo—and the most desperate.

Derek had to assert his authority at once to keep the spies and Judases from being butchered. They may have deserved it, but he could not bring himself to slay a defenseless man, although he knew that Margo scorned such feelings as "impolitic sentimentalism." He just left the three scoundrels gagged and bound on their luxury four-poster.

"The upper story is not far from the surface, Derek," said a spindly little man with only one eye. "But on the surface—"

"Will be nothing to worry you," Derek interrupted. "I myself will lure any Mog nearby to a safe distance. But could you reach the surface before morning?"

"Long before then," he was assured.

Giant swollen tongues of petrified mud, knobby and ash-gray, protruded through the windows along one whole side of the third floor and covered all the stairways to the fourth. The narrow staircase with the strangely grooved metal steps did not reach that high. The workgang had been cutting through one of the tongues, and all their tools lay ready at hand. The name Derek the Hunter was their talisman—whether or not this man with the lantern had any right to it—and they began at once to cut their way toward the roof and freedom.

Whether the petrified mud here was not as solid as it looked, or whether the desperate vigor of the workgang was capable of tearing through any obstacle in its path, it was not many hours before the stairway was reached. At the very center of the top floor, as if a colossal fist had punched its way through the roof, rose a stumpy pillar of rock, a good sixty feet in diameter. But the rest of the floor was undisturbed, and the workgang redoubled its efforts.

Not one man held back; not one man failed to dig as he had never dug before, even under the lash of the Brotherhood of Diablo; not one man—driven, brutalized, desperate—but felt in his heart that he no longer had anything to lose. Their mere lives, condemned to endless drudgery in the quarries, were certainly not worth preserving.

Nor could they long be preserved should the tunnel be detected by a roving Mog. But as they neared the surface Willie always alerted them, by signaling Derek, whenever one was in the neighborhood overhead. Meanwhile he had discovered the toy department. . . .

It was about two hours before dawn when a probing rod finally met with no resistance. Derek stopped the work while he went to collect Willie who, it turned out, had not merely been playing with the toys.

"Watch this, Derek," he cried. "It took me a long time to figure out how it worked."

He set the fluffy toy rabbit on the floor, pushed a

tiny lever, and it began squeaking and hopping up and down.

"It works with wheels and springs," Willie explained. "There's a whole crate of them over there, and I took one apart so I could see how it worked. Now just be patient a minute! There's a Mog roving back and forth right above us, and it never goes more than half a mile away."

"I'll lure it farther away than that," said Derek. "Then these men can join the others and head for our mountain hideaway."

"That's exactly why we'll need these rabbits," Willie cried excitedly. "Now what if the Mog sees one hopping up and down in the moonlight?"

"And then another, and still another?" Derek laughed.

"It might keep him from sounding the alarm. Remember, there's more Mogs roving the neighborhood, because those other buried cities aren't that far away. Once one bellows—for any reason—they all come running."

Derek hesitated, then hefted the big crate of mechanical rabbits. Willie skipped along beside him toward the new tunnel, laughing merrily.

They had to wait nearly half an hour until the roving Mog had reached what seemed to be the most distant point of his rounds. But this gave Derek a chance to send all fifty-four men scurrying through the whole department store after anything that might be used, or later fashioned, as weapons.

"He's almost to where he started coming back the last time," cried Willie, then ducked out of the way while a man-size opening was hacked out of the rock above.

The stars splashed across the cloudless blue-black sky had never shimmered quite so vividly, dimming in luster only where they neared the moon. It was the middle of winter, and the nights were sometimes chilly; but tonight a warm caressing breeze soothed the air from the direction of the New Sea. The landscape itself was less inviting: bald patches of rock mottled with wiry scrub, like the coat of a mangy animal. But whether inviting or not, Willie had to scamper for all he was worth until he and Derek had reached a series of outcrops, directly in the path of the returning Mog.

Ponderously it lumbered into the moonlight—and halted. Not far away it became aware of a strange white object, squeaking and hopping impudently up and down on a rock. After a few moments for the impression to seep into its dull brain, the Mog suddenly lurched forward and smashed the object—only to find an even more impudent white rabbit squeaking and hopping up and down not twenty yards away.

This time it tried to examine the object—only to have it hop right out of its hand. Angrily, the Mog smashed this one too. But there were more, many more; no matter how many it smashed, there always seemed to be one more, and always farther away.

Not until it had been lured a good two miles from its post did it seem uneasy about its surroundings.

"This is the last one," whispered Derek, waiting behind the boulder until he was sure that the Mog was in range before reaching up and pushing the tiny lever.

But as the fluffy white rabbit began to hop mechanically up and down, he heard another squeaking noise directly behind him. Willie lay helplessly on the ground, holding his sides and squeaking with laughter.

"They're so stupid, Derek!" he whispered, barely able to keep his voice down. "Even the wild ones they catch are geniuses compared to Mogs." His squeaks were now louder than those made by the mechanical rabbit on the rock above them.

So loud, in fact, that they were in imminent danger of being detected by the Mog lumbering angrily toward them out of the night. Derek quickly snatched Willie from the ground and carried him, still squeaking with laughter, safely out of range. Even then it took Willie several minutes to compose himself enough to check on the others. These were also out of range now, moving steadily toward the mountain hideaway, guided by Derek's small band of guerillas.

"Then it's time we doubled back ourselves," said Derek. "Is Buck where we left him? All right, let's go. Dawn is beginning to break, and we're still miles from home."

"Oh, look, Derek," cried Willie, as they scrambled down a rugged and scrubby hillside, "the New

Sea. You can just make out the other side from here."

"But not who is there. With all the fleets sent over to raid the coast, it would be a wonder if anybody has survived."

"There's a lot of people there," said Willie. "I know that much. Although I can't tell if they're friends or enemies."

"We must find out soon." Derek shielded his eyes from the morning sunlight, as he gazed across the New Sea. "So we must be ready for any chance of making contact with the Fisherfolk."

"Oh, there's Buck!" cried Willie. "I'm so glad I won't have to walk all the way home now."

Their chance came within less than three weeks, and they were indeed ready for it. Derek now had enough men to keep the Brotherhood of Diablo from concentrating on him alone; and his guerilla bands, operating scores of miles apart, hitting where least expected, continually disorganized any kind of effective pursuit. He was now free to move about the mountainous island almost at will, to take advantage of any opportunity.

The western coast of Diablo was the most treacherous to sail; its convoluted reefs and submerged rocks were considered unnavigable even in daylight, and the black galleys almost never patrolled here after dark especially on moonless nights. The entire gruesome littoral of beetling cliffs and shingle was uninhabited. Perhaps that was why the scout ship of the Fisherfolk had dared anchor here tonight.

It was invisible from shore—to ordinary senses—and not a single light shone on deck. Nor were its approaches defended only by the submerged rocks and shoals.

"The great otter-things are longer than a man," said one of the scouts, a former galley slave that Derek had liberated from the buried city. "Sometimes they would play about our ships when we entered these waters, and the Rathugs would try to gaff them for sport. Once I saw one pulled accidently over the side, and before the other masters could even throw him a line . . ." The man seemed to relish the gruesome details. "Make no hostile gesture, should you meet one, Derek."

"I'll be careful not to," he said drily, as he stripped off his clothes. Whatever dangers awaited him in these dark waters, it might be months before such a chance came again; with the rapidly expanding armaments of the Brotherhood of Diablo, it might never come at all. "Is there anything else that I have to watch out for here?" He was aware that the mysterious forces which had created so many bizarre new species were not confined to the land.

The man considered. "I have heard that there were deadly eels along this coast—ten feet long and as thick as a man's leg—and that they attacked any living thing in the water. But some say that these have disappeared since the coming of the great otter-things." He shrugged. "This I don't know for certain."

Nor did Willie know anything more than there were indeed some strange creatures in the water off shore. All he could do was point his finger directly at the invisible ship.

Derek accordingly set his course by the stars. The surf, breaking over every rock and shoal in its path, marked a clear channel for him; but no man of imagination likes swimming in dark water.

"Don't flash the light until Willie tells you I'm on my way back," he said.

He was barely fifty yards from shore when the first shock hit him. Slimy creatures seemed to swarm all over his body, and for a moment he could think of nothing except deadly eels. But it turned out to be only a bed of kelp, and he was soon through it, swimming with powerful strokes toward a yellow-white star in the constellation of Orion.

Then he saw a large dark object bobbing lazily up and down directly in his path. A log? Flotsam of some kind? He began to veer around it when he was startled to see that the object had a face, a furry clownish face, and that it was watching him. The creature's head was broad and flat, its wide mouth seemed almost to be grinning at him; but it was bigger than he was, and he could only imagine what kind of teeth lay inside that mouth. He was very careful indeed not to make any hostile gesture.

The giant otter-thing lolled on its back; on its chest

lay a succulent meal of shellfish, which it had been cracking open with a rock in its hand-like paw. Derek continued swimming very deliberately toward the yellow-white star.

By the time the ship at last came into sight, he had several of the streamlined creatures—including a cub about the size of Willie—cavorting around him. But other than a few playful whacks with their tails as they dived under him, he was not molested. At last he even came to appreciate their company: neither deadly eels nor any other vicious creature would dare attack him with companions such as these. He hoped they would be waiting for him when he left the ship.

They were, although it was hours later, and a rising wind now drove the surf crashing dangerously over the reefs. They merely found safer channels back to shore, and he followed the gleam of a lantern there as determinedly as he had followed the yellow-white star in Orion.

Chapter 2: The Spies

Winter had been a disappointment to Rollo. He recalled vividly the morning when his father took him to the Gate of Saluston to see the snow; he had only been a child then (he was now going on twelve), but it was an experience that he had never forgotten. Overnight the whole world had turned a beautiful glistening white; the path rimming the Abyss had vanished; even the trees looked misty and unreal. Then the snow mysteriously began to fade. It was all gone before noon, and it never snowed again after that one time.

He had hoped to see more snow this winter; but none came. There had been some rain, the skies tended to be cloudier, and it was sometimes chilly at night; but winter along the shores of the New Sea was not much different from any other season. There was some snow high in the mountains, but even their highest logging camps were well below the snowline.

Otherwise this past winter had been the happiest time of his young life. The shipwrights sent by the Fisherfolk had chased him away at first but he had persisted; hanging around the docks from early morning until late at night; volunteering to sweep up, to carry buckets of tar, anything. At last they let him sharpen some of their tools, then do some rough planing. And he had gone on from there. . . .

He looked proudly at his hands; calloused, stained with pitch and resin, they had grown harder and more dextrous with the passing weeks, gaining all the time in skill and craftsmanship. And the shipwrights had told him many tales of the sea as they worked, of strange lands and peoples that they had seen, of even stranger lands and people of which they had only heard legends. Much of the new earth still lay undiscovered, and now nothing seemed so wonderful to Rollo as to sail a ship beyond the sunset. And he would do it—someday. He was already big for his age. They could not ignore him forever.

This was the first time that he had ever left the job during working hours. Everybody had left the docks the moment that the billowing red and gold sails were sighted rounding the promontory, hurrying to lower the great chain that denied the harbor to enemy ships. Rollo had hurried the other way—not to avoid work, but because he suspected that the ship brought important news.

There had been an unusual amount of activity on the docks these last few weeks—longer working hours, the gathering of stores and provisions, the training of new crews. Something was up, and he was very curious to find out exactly what it was. They were not going to leave him behind this time!

The copse where he had been hiding for nearly two hours now screened him both from above and below; its outlier shrubs grew almost to the walls of the Wise Woman's pavilion. The conference would surely be held right here.

Much had happened since Margo became the Wise Woman. Their fleet was now over fifty strong, prudently scattered in bays and inlets up and down the coast. Their system of watchtowers—signals of smoke by day and fire by night—gave them ample warning of any approaching enemy. Again and again the Brotherhood of Diablo had attacked; once in a massive invasion of over a hundred ships. But they always found the shores deserted. And though they ran their packs of dog-things ragged, they seldom caught anybody. Nor had they ever captured a single ship.

Rollo began to fidget, peeking out every two or three minutes to see if the Wise Woman's litter was yet in sight. His father had been on the dock when the red and gold sails were first sighted—almost as if he had been expecting the ship—and he had immediately sent runners to inform the Wise Woman. That was one reason why he himself had run up the hill and hidden in this copse. He peeked out again.

There she was! Her litter, with twelve bearers at each end, all trained to run in step, rushed up the hillside like a giant centipede. Then Rollo spotted his father shambling along behind the litter, and pulled his head back.

But not before he had noticed that the litter's perch was empty. He feared and distrusted the old witch who usually sat there. His skin crawled whenever he found himself near her—something he always tried to avoid. If anybody would have detected his hiding place, it would have been her. He sighed with relief.

Then they were all inside the pavilion, and he started to creep toward the nearest bush—and instantly dived back again. He should have known there would be a guard! The conference was too important to take any chances; perhaps that was why the old witch had been left behind. Nobody trusted her any more; some even suspected her of being in communication with the Brotherhood of Diablo. But this oaf of a guard was making so much noise that nobody who was not stone deaf could possibly have been caught unawares. Nor did he seem to be looking very hard.

Rollo waited until the guard, stomping noisily through the rough shrubbery, had disappeared around the back of the pavilion. Then he was at the wall with his eye glued to a chink in the warped old logging. He could see over the top of a shelf of books right into the heart of the room.

There stood his father and a dark, wiry little man dressed in a blue shirt and dungarees—the envoy from the Fisherfolk. Margo reposed before them on a fur-covered divan, her face painted in bizarre colors like the old Wise Woman. Rollo had to admit that it did make her look formidable, in a spooky sort of way. He tried to remember that she was just a little girl, even younger than himself.

There were only these three people in the room; but for some reason they all remained silent. Minutes passed, and still not a word was spoken. What were they waiting for?

At last the chief bearer entered the room. "The guard has returned, Your Wisdom. There is nothing unexpected to report." Bowing low, he retired and closed the door behind him.

Rollo saw his father and the envoy from the Fisherfolk exchange quick glances. Even through her bizarre makeup it was obvious that Margo was pleased about something.

"Our flotilla of transport vessels nears completion," she said. "In one month hence we shall be ready to embark. Our victualing by then will have attained a sufficiency. . ."

Rollo did not hear the rest. The sound that alerted him had been very faint, a mere whisper; as if something had brushed lightly against the rear wall of the pavilion. Another guard, stealthier than the first? He crept silently through the shrubbery and peeked around the corner.

The old Wise Woman was pressed against the pavilion wall like a loathesome slug, listening intently to every word spoken inside. The nasty old sneak! What was she doing here? Spying, obviously. But for whom?

Rollo was now in a quandary. He could not warn those inside without also giving himself away. And if the conference ended right now, he would never learn what it was all about. He crept back to his own chink in the wall.

"The tides are a more serious problem near the Great Channel," said the envoy from the Fisherfolk. "Your people are new to the sea, Your Wisdom. The ocean is a far more terrible place than the shallow waters—"

"That will be your responsibility," Margo interrupted. "I am paying you well for your services, and I expect full value in return." She seemed impatient, almost angry.

The man bowed placatingly. "Our covenant will be honorably kept, Your Wisdom. We only wish to make certain that you are fully aware of the risks."

"Hold on a minute," said Gunnar. "I thought that you folks were going to take care of all the risks."

"Precisely," said Margo. "We are to load the first contingent of our people, goods and chattels aboard ship; then proceed through the Great Channel to our settlement in the north, which is beyond the reach of the depredations of the Brotherhood of Diablo. And your own people,'' she added, ''will thus establish a secure and lucrative new market for goods and services. Where are the risks?''

''Do not underestimate the Brotherhood of Diablo, Your Wisdom,'' the envoy cautioned her. ''Our own ships—and yours, which we have helped you build—are designed for speed and handling. They are no match in battle against the great war-galleys of the Brotherhood of Diablo.''

''I don't intend to fight them,'' Margo cried impatiently. ''But to escape them—once and forever. You have promised a diversion to the south, to obviate pursuit. Are you going to tell me now that you are incapable or unwilling to fulfill your obligations?''

''Not at all, Your Wisdom. Our ships will appear in force off the southern coast of Diablo on the very day that your own flotilla is under weigh. But what if the Brotherhood of Diablo is not fooled by our diversion? Their fleet grows in size every day—''

''What are their ungainly hulks to me? You've said yourself that our own ships surpass them in speed and handling.''

''Ah, but that is just the point, Your Wisdom. When you embark for your new settlement in the north, all your ships will be heavily laden with goods and people. Should you be intercepted before you pass through the Great Channel, it might mean disaster. For you could then neither fight nor, perhaps, even outrun the enemy. And if you attempted to return here, they would overwhelm you as you disembarked. That is what I mean by risks, Your Wisdom.''

Margo was silent for several minutes, as if lost in concentration. Rollo watched her even more raptly than his father or the envoy from the Fisherfolk. This was the first he had ever heard about plans for departure to a new settlement; but he understood at once why everything had been kept so secret. He knew from talking to the shipwrights that the Great Channel was the only safe passage out of the New Sea for large vessels. And here was this old witch just around the corner, listening to every word! He was now in more of a quandary than ever.

''I have taken all reasonable precautions to maintain security,'' Margo said at last. ''The inherent risks, I believe, are minimal so long as the Brotherhood of Diablo is unaware of our intentions. And since their nautical razzias have habitually come to naught, they can have no reason to suspect any plans for embarkation. Needless to say, I shall meanwhile redouble my already stringent propugnations.''

The envoy glanced helplessly at Gunnar, who could only gnaw his beard and try not to look utterly bewildered.

Margo continued. ''Then in one month's time, at the dark of the moon—naturally assuming clement weather—I shall embark this first contingent of my people, their goods and chattels. Now what of these precataclysmic structures in the Great Channel?''

''Towers of glass and metal, Your Wisdom. Some

are believed to be inhabited, although by what or whom we don't know. We have never had any reason to investigate. Those that are still standing are plainly visible, even at night. Only those that have collapsed are in any way a hazard to navigation, but we have already arranged to mark them with beacons."

Margo nodded. "Then once my flotilla has cleared the Great Channel, it need only adhere to the northern littoral until it is beyond the reach of the Brotherhood of Diablo. Old Clara Johnson will remain behind to prepare the second and final contingent for embarkation. But what of your own people?"

"We too are concerned with the growing fleet of the enemy, Your Wisdom. When you leave the shores of the New Sea, we ourselves must then bear the brunt of their attacks. Their tribute in men and women has turned even the mountains of the south into a desert."

"Yes," Margo said dispassionately, "a curious example of the institutionalization of practices associated historically only with times of siege or famine. What may have been a matter of survival in the years subsequent to the cataclysm has evolved into an established economy. I regret that our impending embarkation precludes my studying it in any appreciable detail. But I believe that you were commenting on the response of your own people to impending challenges by the Brotherhood of Diablo?"

The envoy blinked. "Uh, yes, Your Wisdom. We will be challenged indeed, for, as you know, the

Rathagon has declared the subjection of all peoples who still deny him tribute. When we can no longer maintain ourselves on our northern islands—and, I fear, that time will not be long in coming—then we too must seek a refuge beyond the reach of the Brotherhood of Diablo. But this will not prevent our fulfilling every letter of our covenant with Your Wisdom. Our Council has sent me here specifically to assure you of this."

"Then I have no further animadversions upon our general strategy. Gunnar?"

He frowned and tugged at his beard and wiped his big paw across his forehead. "Sounds good to me."

Margo said, "Perhaps we should refresh ourselves before proceeding to the logistical details of our forthcoming embarkation. Gunnar, please inform the man waiting at the door."

He nodded and left the room. Rollo alone noticed the sly look in his eye.

The next thing he knew he was again diving for cover. Maybe the guard would catch the old hag this time—and solve his quandary for him. But, no. The oaf was making more noise than ever. Rollo watched him disappear around the rear of the pavilion.

Then he had the idea of informing one of the guards or litter-bearers. If they caught the old hag in the act of spying, they probably wouldn't ask too many questions about his own presence up here. He might even get a reward. In any case, he had already heard everything there was to hear. Everything important, anyway.

He crept back to the rear of the pavilion again; the moment the old hag resumed her spying, he would hurry and fetch witnesses. But she did not return. He waited ten minutes, then twenty. After half an hour he finally gave up; she was not coming back at all. Perhaps she no longer had any need to—after all, she had heard everything that he had. What was he going to do now?

It was late afternoon and the briny tang of the air softened into a twilight aroma of pine, wildflowers and the elusive muskiness of decaying vegetation. A tiny blue-green lizard hopped on two legs across Rollo's path as he entered the forest; the muskiness of decay grew stronger, the shadows deeper. He noticed an animal trap; it was still empty.

He wandered deeper and deeper into the forest. The farms of the local people had become more efficient since Margo became the Wise Woman; hunting, trapping, and fishing had also prospered. Although nobody seemed to know what had happened to Derek the Hunter. More and more people were saying that he was dead, or captured by the Brotherhood of Diablo. And his woman Eva? And Jana? Not that he had at all missed the latter. . . .

Suddenly he turned on his heel, hopped quickly from stone to stone as he recrossed a stream, and marched decisively back through the dark aisles of trees and ferns. He could see the pavilion silhouetted against the darkening rose-violet of sunset. Was his father still there? Had the old hag crept back by another route and rejoined Margo? He hesitated for a moment.

At last he marched on more decisively than ever. Even if it got him punished, somebody had to be told. What if they sailed for this new refuge and found the entire fleet of the Brotherhood of Diablo waiting for them in the Great Channel? What was a scolding, or even a beating, compared to that?

He had hoped to get into the pavilion without being recognized by the sentinels. But he was handled roughly; one insolent litter-bearer even shoved him off the veranda. Then he had no choice but to identify himself as Gunnar's son.

This had a remarkable effect. The man who took his message into the pavilion was suddenly very polite about it; there was no more harassment by those who remained outside.

"Sorry about that, kid," apologized the man who had shoved him off the veranda. "Just doing our job, that's all. You understand how it is."

"Better hope his old man understands how it is," said another litter-bearer, and they all laughed.

Although the pavilion now overlooked the New Sea, it had apparently stood well inland before the cataclysm; perhaps a mountain lodge of some kind. A vestibule and two small bedrooms flanked a large hall of rough-hewn timber. Bookshelves rose in precise tiers and all the furniture was arranged with mathematical exactitude. But there was a cheerful fire and plenty of candles.

Rollo found it easier to explain what happened than he had expected. Margo had washed the bizarre paint from her face, and wore only a simple green robe. And although she watched him with a strange intentness, he was able to remember that she was after all just a young girl. He hid nothing.

She did not seem at all surprised to hear that the sneaking old hag had been spying on her. "But you did not return by yourself after old Clara Johnson left the vicinity?"

"No, I just wandered around for a couple of hours, wondering what I should do."

She looked searchingly at him, her eyes glittering with cold calculation. Suddenly she rose and left the hall. For a nervous moment he was afraid that she had gone to summon an executioner.

But she returned alone, and a few minutes later a servant entered with a tray of food. His stomach began to growl, and he now remembered that he had not eaten since breakfast. The excitement had at least not spoiled his appetite.

Then he had another nervous idea. He had heard rumors that people who opposed the Wise Woman were not executed, they just disappeared. It struck him now that she had not been at all disturbed that he knew her secret plans for embarkation. Was it because it no longer mattered what he knew? Was this his last meal? For a moment he found it hard to swallow.

And why was she watching him so curiously? She had been reading when he entered; there were stacks of books on either side of her, one coming and one going. She still nestled on her fur-covered divan, as if prepared to resume her studies the moment she disposed of his body. But when she finally spoke it was not his death sentence. In fact, he hardly understood a thing that she said.

"We are still children in years, but judging from your somatic structure you will someday be at least as large and powerful a man as your father. Although, it is to be hoped, not as hairy." There was a calculating look in her eyes. "My own impending biological efflorescence, assuming the usual dimorphic rates of pubescent metamorphosis, will accrue concomitantly with your own."

He blinked at her. "Uh, these cookies are very good."

She continued to appraise him intently for several minutes, while he continued to empty the tray. She still had not told him how she would deal with his information, or even if she believed him. But this was evidently not his last meal after all.

"You must not repeat to anyone else what you have told me here tonight," she said. "Not even to your father."

"Don't worry about that," he assured her.

Then he found himself backing awkwardly from the room, never able to take his eyes from hers. She seemed to trust his keeping everything that he had seen or heard today strictly to himself, which was very reassuring. And she really was kind of cute in a way. Something like a hungry cat.

Chapter 3: The Voyage to Diablo

Jana watched Eva in silence for several moments, a puzzled expression on her little face. She despaired of ever comprehending the bizarre relationships between men and women in matters of love; although she had a very discerning eye for everything else human, especially the ridiculous side. How much simpler was her own relationship with Willie—they were both exactly alike in all things!

"You'll start talking like Margo pretty soon, Eva," she observed at last, "if you keep reading so many books."

She smiled. "Just so long as I don't start thinking like Margo. She sent me most of these books, by the way."

"What's that one called?"

"It's by an admiral named Mahan—*The Influence of Sea-Power Upon History*. The important thing I've learned is that the strategy for boats with motors is the same as that for galleys, because neither is dependent upon the volume or direction of the wind to maneuver."

Their room in the village of the Fisherfolk was snug and shipshape; the only clutter was a heap of books, some rather musty and water-stained. Jana opened two or three at random, but none of the illustrations was very attractive. Just a lot of diagrams, with rows of black rectangles facing rows of white rectangles, and arrows going every which way. She had liked the illustrations in Derek's books at Saluston much better—and the stories he sometimes read to them.

"Weren't you happy when you heard that Derek was still alive?" she said at last. "I mean, so happy that you felt like singing, or just leaping up and down for joy?"

"Or sitting for hours with my forehead against the wall, laughing and hugging myself?" added Eva, and they both laughed, for that had been exactly Jana's reaction to the good news. "It was different for you, because you at least knew that Willie was still alive."

"But I didn't know if the Rathugs had caught him and put him in a cage again, and stuck him with sharp needles and kept him awake all night, the way they used to. I was never happier in my life when that sea-captain with the fuzzy beard brought news that they were both still alive and safe."

Eva smiled whimsically. "Yes, I felt the same way."

"But you didn't show it very much. You just started reading these fat musty books all day and night, and copying out illustrations, and making charts, and so forth."

Eva took the little creature affectionately into her arms. "There are more ways of showing happiness, dear, than laughing and talking to ourselves for hours on end. I'm just doing everything I can to make sure they remain alive and safe. But I'll never be really happy, and neither will Derek, until everybody in the world is safe from the Brotherhood of Diablo."

"You've been sending messages back and forth with Margo, haven't you? Are we going to fight the Brotherhood of Diablo?"

"That depends upon events on Diablo itself."

"But how do we know what's going on there? Derek only sent word about things like boats with motors, like the ones taken from Saluston, and cannons, those tubes that shoot metal balls at you with a loud noise, and big smoky buildings where they make such things. And that the Rathugs have their poor slaves working night and day."

"Now you know why we must also work night and day, both here and back on the mainland."

"Oh, we don't have to worry about Margo putting people to work," Jana said disgustedly. "But at least she kept everybody from being caught when the Brotherhood of Diablo raided there. She's always been good at traps and surprises."

"But with no real flair for grand strategy, I'm afraid," said Eva. "A wise old general once said, 'In war, there is no substitute for victory.' Margo is brilliant at devising tactics, but her overall strategy tends to be confused with too many substitutes for victory."

"I sometimes think we'd all be more comfortable with a substitute for Margo," muttered Jana. "Does she know what's happening on Diablo?"

"Only Derek and Willie know that, dear."

Jana sighed. "A lot of good that does us! Oh, I wish there was some way we could find out what's happening to them!"

"Well, I suppose the best way of doing that is just to go there and ask them," Eva said quietly.

But Jana's reaction was anything but quiet. Even at the meeting of the Council the next afternoon she still tended to behave like an excited and happy child—which is just what the body of stern old sea-captains thought her to be, in any case.

Eva made no attempt to disillusion them. She sensed how little disposed such men were to admit a woman in their counsels at all—even the woman of Derek the Hunter—and any explanation about Jana would probably have just made them even less disposed to trust her.

The Council chamber of the Fisherfolk was also

snug and shipshape; surrounded by a hull, it could have sailed straight out to sea. The manner in which Eva herself sailed straight at every proposal or objection at last won her the confidence of the Council members. By the time they adjourned, she was no longer regarded as merely the woman of Derek the Hunter.

Yet she had not missed the exchange of sly looks when it was determined that the captain with whom Derek had first made contact was the most reliable man to carry her and her little mascot back to Diablo. But if there was some unknown problem there, she prudently allowed the Council itself to work it out.

Nor did they dawdle. By the time she and Jana had walked the length of the village's single street—objects of gawking curiosity every step of the way—they found a messenger from the Council already climbing into a longboat at the wharf.

"Which is our ship?" asked Jana.

"Probably one of the galleys over there, tied to the top story of that submerged building."

"There's a whole city underwater, isn't there?" Jana shielded her eyes from the late afternoon sun. "The longboat is rowing straight down one of the streets." She burst into merry laughter. "Now it's turning the corner."

"I believe some of the drowned buildings almost reach the surface," said Eva, "and might tear the bottom of a boat. Those where the fleet is tied up must have been the tallest buildings in the city, right at its very center. But we'd better get to work—we're leaving in the morning."

"Are you going to be in charge?" said Jana, skipping along at her side as they turned back toward their quarters.

"Just of the overall mission. The captain, of course, will be in charge of the ship itself."

"The same captain who brought the news, the one with the big fuzzy beard?" She burst merrily into laughter. "I don't think he's going to like it very much."

The captain tugged discontentedly at the bush concealing the lower half of his face. He was a leathery and weather-salted little man; a confirmed bachelor who habitually ranked women only by their varying degrees of tiresomeness. This was to be his second perilous voyage to Diablo in just three months; a voyage whose difficulties challenged even the most experienced sailors, and which still called for as much luck as skill in order to succeed. He was very discontented indeed to find himself placed under the command of a woman.

He had seriously considered refusing the commission. But the Council had at last prevailed upon him, commending his proven skill and experience, assuring him that he was the only captain among the Fisherfolk who could be depended on to succeed in so risky a voyage, appealing in every way to his vanity and professional pride. Nor was he left in doubt about the vital importance of the voyage.

So now he found himself about to convey the woman of Derek the Hunter and her little mascot all the way back to Diablo, with the understanding that he would obey her every direction concerning the route—no matter how strange it might seem.

His first voyage, three months ago, had been strange enough. He had been on scouting missions before; but never so close to Diablo, especially so close to the treacherous western coast of the island. But he felt reasonably secure. No patrol galley would risk these waters on a moonless night, and he could easily outrun the clumsy hulks during daylight. He was anchored amidst a veritable sea-fortress of reefs and shoals, a good mile from shore. It was unlikely that anybody on Diablo could even see him.

Then, about two hours after midnight, he was astonished to find a strange man on deck.

The legend of Derek the Hunter had already begun to fade at that time; more and more people believed that he had been killed or, perhaps even worse, captured alive by the Brotherhood of Diablo. A few had even begun to wonder if there had really ever been such a person. But there he stood: naked, alone, drenched by the waves and spindrift. It was a mystery how he even knew that the ship was here, let alone reached it from shore. Eeriest of all, the watch reported seeing several dark shapes larger than a man cavorting through the water below.

But although the captain was truly astonished—something it took a great deal to do—he had been at sea too many years not to know his duty. Having a blanket fetched for Derek the Hunter, and hot drinks for both of them, he led the way to his cabin, where he kept his official log under lock and key. Only here, with the door closed and curtains drawn, did he dare light even a candle.

He heard many startling things about the Brotherhood of Diablo; about their insane build-up of armaments; about the island of Diablo itself. Derek the Hunter was naturally relieved to learn that his woman was safe with the Fisherfolk, along with her little mascot; and he dictated messages for them. The captain diligently recorded every word in his log, which he resolved not to let out of his sight until he dutifully handed it over to the Council.

Then the entire crew watched in astonishment as Derek the Hunter plunged fearlessly into the midst of the dark shapes cavorting below—and just vanished. Nobody on deck could honestly say that they even saw him break the surface again. But soon a gleam of light appeared on shore, and consternation at once gave way to caution.

The first rays of dawn found the ship already working its way through the labyrinthine rocks and shoals toward the open sea. Its scouting mission had officially just begun; but not a man in the crew failed to guess that their gravest duty now was to race home with the news as fast as their fleet galley could ply the seas.

The captain again tugged discontentedly at his bushy beard as he recalled the reward for all his diligence—another perilous voyage to Diablo, under the command of a woman.

The harbor around him stood at the very heart of a ring of islands; there were so many escape channels leading from the New Sea that only a great armada of hundreds of enemy ships could have hoped to bottle up the fleet of the Fisherfolk. Nor could any but a few of the ships have been surprised from land; for most of them were tied up at the center of the basin, where the upper storys of a cluster of drowned buildings broke the surface. It was many years since the Brotherhood of Diablo had raided here, and the rebuilt fishing village now housed well over a thousand people.

As the captain watched the noisy, excited crowd approaching the dock, he recalled some of the things that Derek the Hunter had told him about the Brotherhood of Diablo's great armada. He knew that the Fisherfolk had survived as a free people only because their ships had thus far been too elusive for the ponderous war-galleys of the enemy. But ships driven by motor! With cannon!

That was the main reason why he had at last accepted this mortifying commission. Although he still could not see any possible usefulness in the voyage. Did they expect Derek the Hunter to swim out to the ship again? How could he even know that a ship was coming? Or where it would anchor?

He gave his bushy beard another impatient tug. It was the growing of that beard that had made his career possible. Few now remembered what a ridiculous figure he had cut as a youth; none knew of the ointments he had secretly smeared on the lower half of his face—such as it was. Many had been born more badly marked than himself; but no leader of men can afford to look comical, even ridiculous. His face was devoid of a chin; ending in a pendulous lower lip. Even the twisted and deformed had laughed at him.

But now he had a beard; a full, bushy, masterful beard. Tugging at it in times of doubt or pressure was a habit with him, as if reassuring himself that it was still there. He tugged at it now as he watched the two figures, surrounded by the entire population of the town, moving down the quay. The woman carried the little girl on her shoulders.

Eva stopped at the foot of the gangplank; she put Jana down and briefly addressed the crowd. After a few parting words with members of the Council, she took Jana's hand and started up the gangplank. At that moment she met the captain's eye. The look jolted him like a charge of static electricity, and for several moments he was completely unable to speak or move or even turn his eyes away.

Eva was dressed in the blue shirt and dungarees of the Fisherfolk, but she still somehow managed to appear half naked. Jana wore a scaled-down version of the same costume, and her eyes twinkled with merriment as she noticed the captain's reaction. He said something gruff, which may have been meant to welcome them aboard, and at last turned away and began shouting orders.

But his crew had also noticed the passengers and were slow to take their stations. This did not improve the captain's temper. He had expected a troublesome voyage, but he would do his duty—and so would his crew! Shouting, growling, cursing, barking orders left and right, he tugged at his beard as if trying to tear it out by the roots. He got the ship smartly under weigh, and soon they were beating their way down the channel toward the New Sea.

He had naturally assumed that they would try to make contact with Derek the Hunter about where he had swum out to the ship before. Thus he had set their course and time of departure so that they would not pass through the Great Channel until nightfall. They could then lie safely off the western coast until late the following afternoon, which might give Derek the Hunter at least a chance of spotting them; then anchor among the rocks and shoals just before dark. But trouble began for the captain even sooner than he had expected.

He had been glad to see the little girl behaving herself; the voyage was too dangerous to be bothered with troublesome brats. All the while that they coasted the northern islands she had sat quietly by herself, her little head tilted slightly to one side. It was just before sunset that she summoned the woman to her—and the woman in turn summoned him. She told him that they were going the wrong way.

Her directions were necessarily vague, but a lifetime of scouting and fishing voyages had given him a sound knowledge of Diablo, its offshore rocks and shoals, its beetling cliffs and promontories. He recognized at once a remote corner of northeastern Diablo, where sheer cliffs rose a thousand feet out of the sea. There would be no swimming out to the ship along that coast, nor any place where he could land so much as a rowboat.

But it is a hard thing for a bachelor to argue with a beautiful and voluptuous young woman—even when he knows better. And the captain certainly did know better in this case; there was no possible way of making contact with anybody in that remote corner of the island. Nonetheless he reset his course. For once the Council had been right. They had warned him that the woman's orders might seem rather strange.

He gave his beard a savage tug, and stomped the length of the ship. A strong current flowed in through the Great Channel, and they would now be taking it abeam; the handling of the ship would be rough and treacherous. He took the wheel himself.

Trouble now began for Jana. The setting sun illuminated a strange sunken world of ruined cities, of wave-lashed towers of brick and stone; miles to the west could be seen the silhouettes of even greater towers. There were whole towns beneath the sea, and Jana stood on an inverted bucket at the rail, gazing down at them in wonder. Then suddenly she did not feel very good.

The current pouring into the New Sea was strong and choppy, and the galley began to roll queasily back and forth. Soon Jana felt so miserable that she could hardly balance herself on the bucket. Then her supper was gone, and she laid her little head on the rail and moaned. She knew that she was going to die; at the moment she didn't really care.

Eva carried her to the stern of the ship and laid her gently on a blanket. She returned a few minutes later with some dry biscuits; she made Jana eat two of these, and ate some herself.

Then Jana realized that Eva did not look very good either; she was pale, with an unusual tightness about her mouth, and she swallowed too often. There was a look of determination on her face, however, and she chewed each biscuit very slowly.

The captain was too busy fighting the current to bother with them, but several of his crew were now hanging over the railings, and those still at their oars were unable to make much headway. Jana noticed this, and she ate another biscuit and began to feel better.

The pale sliver of the moon set only an hour after sundown; but the night was cloudless, and glittering splashes of stars streamed across the sky. They were out of the Great Channel now, and Jana found it easier to concentrate. Eva carried her directions to the captain, who resignedly reset his course. That it only brought them at last beneath a sheer wall of rock, which loomed over a thousand feet above them, did not seem to surprise him. He sighed and had the anchor dropped. There was no possible way of getting any closer.

"We may have to wait an hour or two," said Eva.

The captain merely nodded, and stared fixedly up at the mast for several minutes. Then he left the entire stern of the ship to the woman and the little girl to sit grumpily at the bow, his beard grasped firmly in both hands. He was happy that it was too dark to see what was happening at the other end of the ship.

In fact, nothing happened for over two hours. Then Jana suddenly became excited, and Eva actually had to hold her to keep her from dancing up and down. For the next hour they spoke in whispers, interspersed with short or long silences.

Most of the crew were asleep by now; their snores drowned by the crash of the surf against the looming cliff wall.

The captain did not sleep, however; he never did this close to Diablo. Nor did the rhythmic crashing of the surf even make him drowsy; he was too well aware that a single storm wave could batter them to pieces against that same cliff wall. He gave up even guessing why they were anchored here. He had come across many weird beings during an adventurous life, but none that could climb down a thousand feet of sheer rock and then swim through a good half mile of pounding surf. Nothing could reach them here from the land.

The sea was another matter. With all that he had heard about cannons and boats with motors, he was determined to weigh anchor before dawn—no matter what orders he got from the woman, even if she was beautiful and voluptuous, and her eyes seemed to loosen his knee joints every time she looked at him.

For all he knew there were cannons trained on them from the top of the cliff right now, ready to fire at the first light of dawn. Since he had never actually seen either a cannon or a boat with a motor, he found the prospect of confronting them very alarming indeed.

Then he realized that the woman was approaching him from the stern of the ship. He rose stiffly to his feet, determined to resist any orders that might keep them in these waters after dawn. But she only said:

"We can go back now."

"Then this whole voyage was a waste," he muttered, not without a touch of satisfaction.

"Not at all. I have urgent news for the Council, so we must return with all possible speed."

The captain started to reply, but then just grumbled, "Oh, we'll get back home fast enough, don't worry about that." And he stomped up and down the benches, kicking his crew awake.

Recrossing the Great Channel was not so queasy

an experience this time, and even Jana managed to hold on to her breakfast.

Dawn found her and Eva talking and laughing excitedly together at the stern rail. The captain stood resolutely at the wheel nearby, but he could not keep his eyes from drifting toward Eva from time to time. The sparkle of excitement in her eyes enhanced her already striking beauty.

Taking advantage of a southwest breeze, the homeward voyage was indeed faster than the voyage out. Eva thanked the captain for his diligence so graciously that he could only follow her down the gangplank with longing eyes.

Not many weeks passed before he was no longer a bachelor; married to a rather long-faced woman (attracted perhaps by her prominent chin), he was soon on the road to becoming a family man in a big way.

Chapter 4: Colinga Harbor

Willie applied the ointment very gingerly to Buck's muzzle. The mineshaft had been occupied when they first discovered it, and the great beast had been sent in as usual to handle the eviction. But this time he had been surprised. The big cat-thing had fought him standing on its hind legs, with a quickness that was almost supernatural; and he had been well clawed before his greater weight and strength finally prevailed. He sullenly accepted Willie's doctoring, although the ointment stung his nose.

It was the dark of the moon, and they both preferred the open air at the entrance of the mineshaft. Willie found his range of perception rather constricted underground, and Buck did not like all the bright torches down there.

Colinga Harbor lay only a few miles down the coast. The raid now being organized was the most daring that they had ever attempted—and the most important. A whole fleet was awaiting their signal, somewhere out on the New Sea.

Willie already knew what they were going to do—or, at least, try to do. It still seemed rather desperate to him. Nearly a month had passed since he and Jana had come close enough to communicate, and all the plans made then would at last be carried out tonight. He hoped.

Somehow the Brotherhood of Diablo had been led to believe that the Wise Woman's people were planning to try and escape them. He knew that they had already sent their main fleet to block the Great Channel. Then their auxiliary fleet was supposed to sweep out of Colinga Harbor and catch the escaping fleet from behind like giant pincers. And none of the Wise Woman's ships would be able to get away, because there were ships at Colinga Harbor with motors. Which meant that they were very fast.

He had no mechanical aptitude whatsoever, and did not really understand all the strategy that he and Jana had transmitted to each other nearly a month ago. But it all seemed more desperate than ever. Very gently he smoothed more stinging ointment across Buck's muzzle.

The sea had come here only within the memory of living men, but many of the cliffs below had already been undercut, and here and there could be seen patches of open beach. Tons of abrasives—rocks, pebbles, coarse sand—were hurled again and again at the rugged coast, and each retreating wave carried back with it a part of the land. The ceaseless pounding could be heard faintly even in the lowest shafts of the mine.

Torches blazed in the main gallery, far underground. This was the first time that all the guerilla bands had gathered in one place, and they listened eagerly as their leader addressed them.

"After tonight's work we'll all have to go into hiding for a while," said Derek. "Maybe for a long while. You know why they haven't bothered with us these last couple of months. But they'll be bothering us a lot after tonight's work, you can be sure of that."

There was some nervous laughter. Not a man present but showed the marks of recent captivity; Derek himself bore a new scar across his left arm and shoulder, inflicted on him by a monstrous Rathug (now deceased). But the Brotherhood of Diablo had mysteriously stopped all pursuit, although surely by this time the Rathagon knew that the guerilla bands harrying his outposts all over Diablo were led by Derek the Hunter.

Eva had seen this as certain proof that he had heard about the supposed flight of the Wise Woman's people, that he was concentrating all his efforts on the armada that was to intercept them. Why else was Derek the Hunter on Diablo but as a diversion? Once the escaping fleet was captured, then the Rathagon could turn and hunt down his most intolerable enemy at his leisure; perhaps even recover Willie alive.

All Derek's subsequent actions had been aimed at confirming this belief. Again and again he had raided those outposts farthest from the Great Channel; but the Rathagon had refused to divert so much as a single platoon to hunt him down. That would come later.

The island fortifications had not been built to keep enemies out, but to keep slaves in. Derek had learned from escaped slaves that there were no defenses at all protecting Colinga Harbor.

"Stay away from the roads," he continued. "The trucks are now being used to service the fleets. But after tonight they'll be used to hunt us down. And don't worry about communication. No matter how remote your hiding place, I'll find you when I need you."

The men nodded and exchanged glances. None doubted any more that their leader really was Derek the Hunter; now they knew that this was not just another doomed gesture of despair, and they began to dream great dreams. Perhaps the Brotherhood of Diablo was not invincible after all. Although every man in the crowded gallery realized that after tonight, whether they succeeded or failed, they would be hunted as no living creature on Diablo had ever been hunted before. All knew better than to be captured alive.

"Always remember," said Derek, "that our purpose is to destroy, not fight. That will come later. Now I know that you're tired, that we're all tired, that we've been on the march since before dawn—"

"And for two days before that," somebody cried.

"Yes, but that only means we won't be expected on this side of the island. They think we're still raiding plantations a hundred miles away."

At that moment one of the scouts entered the gallery and pushed his way forward. He started to whisper the report, but Derek shook his head.

"Tell them all. Let nothing be hidden from anyone."

"Slaves is going aboard ship," reported the scout. "Already chaining 'em to their oars. Lots of fussing around them boats with motors."

Derek glanced significantly at a picked band of about forty men standing to his right. They nodded: the boats with motors would not leave Colinga Harbor tonight—perhaps never.

"Not much sign of Rathugs yet," continued the scout. "Looks like Derek was right again. They won't be leaving till the middle of the night, maybe even dawn."

Derek clapped him on the back. "Good work. For the rest of you, I can only say good luck. Any last questions? Then let's get going."

Buck wrinkled his nose at the reek of gasoline, then growled because it was still sore. Willie got him out of the way as the men filed silently up out of the mineshaft and disappeared into the chaparral. Some night creature howled eerily in the darkness nearby. Buck growled again.

"He's still in a bad mood," said Willie, as Derek emerged from the mine. "And I don't much like those nasty-smelling bottles either. Phew!"

"The Rathugs at Colinga Harbor will like them even less. Anybody around?"

Willie did not tilt his head slightly to one side the way Jana did, but leaned forward as if contemplating his navel. His powers of perception seemed just as acute, however.

"Nothing we have to worry about," he reported at last. "I think the creature making all the noise over there in the scrub is some kind of dog-thing. Maybe he smells those nasty bottles too." He started to climb onto Buck's back but changed his mind. "I think I'd better walk for a while. I've never seen him in such a bad mood before."

"He'll be all right once the fighting starts," said Derek. "In fact, he may want to fight too much. Be sure you get him out of Colinga Harbor the minute you hear the signal—no matter who or what he's fighting at the time."

"I'll try," Willie said doubtfully. As with Jana, Buck trusted his senses but not his judgment; nor did he always obey him. "What are you listening for?"

"Bottles."

"Bottles? I don't hear anything."

The old roadway ran straight to the edge of the cliff; the ruins of tumbled-down buildings loomed in the darkness on either side. Derek helped Willie scramble over a fissure in the contorted pavement. Buck padded sullenly behind.

"I don't hear anything either," Derek said at last. "With hundreds of bottles in those cases, the clinking of just a few of them could give us away. The sound travels a long distance. That's why I had all the cases stuffed with rags."

"And the bottles are stuffed with rags too," said Willie. "I saw them—and smelled them. Phew! They smell worse than those nasty trucks that chase us down the roads. But won't there be dog-things at Colinga Harbor?"

"Probably. Why?"

"Well, if I can smell those bottles, they'll certainly be able to, maybe miles away. I don't think it's the clinking we have to worry about."

"There will be a lot more nasty smells near Colinga Harbor, smells even worse than the gasoline in those bottles. Remember what I told you about the machines and foundries there? And you already know about the trucks. Well, most of them run on gasoline."

"Do they get it from the back of rusty automobiles, the way we do?"

"I think they've discovered some old storage tanks at Colinga Harbor. Or built them. In any case, it's not just a matter of siphoning off enough gasoline to fill a few hundred old wine and beer bottles. Their storage tanks hold thousands and thousands of gallons. They should make a good beacon for our fleet, and it doesn't matter how many machines they have if there's no fuel to run them."

"Jana was right about your being smart," said Willie. "Although she doesn't think you're as smart as this Margo person."

"Nobody is," said Derek, laughing. "But I think it's time you started riding. There are the lights of Colinga Harbor just down the coast. Here, Buck!"

Colinga Harbor was an inundated mountain valley; broad and shallow, it narrowed to a channel less than two hundred feet across where it entered the New Sea. Fault scarps, flooded chasms, and other signs of cataclysmic earth movements were everywhere; but the basin itself, like a dusty mirror, reflected the stars and the lanterns of a hundred ships riding at anchor. Only shouts and drunken laughter from the dockside taverns and the occasional yapping of a dog-thing broke through the throbbing metallic clangor of the shops and foundries.

They approached the town along the shingle right at the water's edge, a file of dark shapes silhouetted against the mirror-like basin of the harbor. Cases of bottles were suspended from a score of carrying poles, but there was not a sound. Willie checked continually for patrols or hidden guard-posts, but found none.

"I see what you mean about the smells," he whispered. "Buck doesn't like them either, and now he's got his paws wet. I've never seen him in such a nasty mood."

Derek examined the great beast. "I think you're

right. He's obviously spoiling for a fight, and there's no reason now for either of you to enter the town. Maybe it would be better . . . See the base of that promontory over there?''

''The one that stretches across the harbor entrance?''

''Yes, that's it. According to the scouts, there's a grove of dwarf oaks near the sea. That's where we'll meet.''

''You mean circle all the way around? But how will you be able to cross the harbor?''

''By ship,'' said Derek. He squatted down and hugged Buck and scratched his ears. The great beast wagged his tail a few times but there was no doubt that he really was in a bad mood. Willie would never be able to control him once the fighting started. ''We'll do as much damage as we can, but the important thing is to keep any ships from leaving the harbor tonight. Especially those with motors. I'll meet you in the grove of oaks as soon as I can. Go on, Buck! Go on, now!''

Buck raised his huge green eyes for a moment, then turned and padded sullenly back down the shingle. Willie gave a quick little wave, then dug his fingers into Buck's shaggy coat and held tight.

A hundred men may destroy a city if they are determined and resourceful enough. These were the pick of all the guerilla bands on Diablo, and Derek had assigned their leaders to deal with the storage tanks—the most difficult and treacherous assignment of all. He himself would lead the boarding parties.

Bottles of gasoline, their necks stuffed with flammable rags, were distributed among those entering the town itself; each band of men carried a shuttered lantern, and they slipped away into the darkness by various paths.

Derek's men carried axes, along with their usual weapons. The rowboats were just where the scouts had said they would be, and they boarded them silently and pushed off from shore. Two ships would be enough, but Derek chose the very largest and heaviest galleys in the entire harbor. The Brotherhood of Diablo had done them a service by efficiently chaining up their galley slaves so many hours in advance. Efficiency sometimes works against itself.

The reflected stars and lanterns were now distorted by ripples; but the noise of the foundries, echoing across the mirror-like stillness of the harbor, drowned out the splash of the oars. Then the water began to brighten, and cries of alarm began to penetrate even the throbbing metallic clangor of the town. Derek kept his men rowing at a steady pace.

The two ponderous galleys were anchored at the very center of the harbor; if any of the smaller ships noticed the rowboats filtering among them, there was no alarm. At least, none from the ships themselves. The galley slaves of the Brotherhood of Diablo were generally so dispirited that only a token watch was needed to guard them. If these few watchmen were now alarmed about anything, it was the growing noise and light and confusion in the town. Derek kept his men moving steadily.

Then they reached the first of the two galleys; Derek led the boarding party over the bulwarks and onto the deck. The two watchmen were easily overpowered. Meanwhile the second boarding party had reached its own galley and was scrambling aboard. Pillars of flame now rose from several parts of the town; the metallic clangor died away amidst an uproar of shouting and screaming, the angry bellowing of commands. The waters of the harbor no longer reflected the stars.

"Unlock them while we move," cried Derek. He took the ring of keys from the chief watchman and tossed it to one of his men. "Slip the anchor chain! You men with the axes, take your positions! Let's go!"

The galley slaves were too terrified not to obey, and the ponderous hulk began to edge slowly toward the narrow mouth of the harbor. The docks were now a curtain of flame; several of the boats with motors were burning, although there was still no sign of fire from the direction of the gasoline storage tanks. Then the second galley also left its moorings.

"Are all the men unchained?" cried Derek. "Then start cutting through the hull! Helmsman, to port! Straight across the narrows of the channel!"

The hacking chuff of the axes seemed to echo the pandemonium raging from the town. Derek saw with satisfaction that the other galley was also beginning to pivot as it entered the narrow channel. Then there were frightened cries all along the benches, and several slaves leapt to their feet. The bilges were beginning to fill with water.

"Stay at your oars!" he cried. "We'll get you all safely off the ship! Becker, Lopez, get ready to rig a line to shore! All right, bring her around!" he shouted to the helmsman. "Right across the entrance!"

As the men began rigging a line to shore, Derek snatched up an axe and began chopping still another hole through the hull-planks. The bilges were already knee deep, and water gushed in around him faster and faster. The ponderous hulk slowly settled directly athwart the channel.

"All right, one bench at a time!"

There was no pushing or shoving; not the least sign of panic. The galley slaves moved as abjectly as cattle, bench by bench, over the side, pulling themselves along the line rigged to shore. Then they just sat down and waited.

"Lopez, take charge of them!" cried Derek, half in pity, half in disgust at their submission. "Get them out of here and keep them moving!"

There was a heavy groaning thunk as the keel hit bottom. Water was now pouring in over the bulwarks and Derek grabbed the nearest railing and started to vault over the side. Then he became aware of a pathetic wailing aboard the second galley. That ship had also begun to settle in the water, completely blocking the harbor entrance; it would now take the

Brotherhood of Diablo days, perhaps weeks, to clear the channel. But the slaves aboard were still chained to their oars.

He leaped for the riggings, swung himself to the stern rail, and plunged into the sea. A few powerful strokes brought him alongside the galley; hand over hand he climbed one of the oars and scrambled on deck. The water flooding the bilges was already waist high, and the galley slaves wailed and tugged futilely at their chains.

"Unlock them!" Derek cried angrily.

"No keys!" replied one of his men. They had all moved toward the bow and were just preparing to abandon ship. "The chief watchman jumped overboard and swam for shore the minute he seen us. Tried hacking through the chains, but only split the axe. Nothing we could do about it, Derek."

"Chop the staples out of the bulkhead!" cried Derek. "Hurry! Longboats are beginning to leave the docks. Here, you two. Start rigging lines to shore. Heavy lines. These men will have to carry their chains with them."

The chuff of axes sounded all about him as he splashed and clambered to the starboard railing. Half the foundries and warehouses were now ablaze; all but three of the boats with motors were burning in the water; the entire harbor basin now glowed like amber. Rathugs and slaves could be seen reeling and staggering along the docks, running madly back and forth through the flames, screaming and cursing and dying. But he counted nine longboats, fully manned with Rathugs, driving ominously toward them through the fleet.

The ease with which he had captured the first two galleys had momentarily encouraged him to wonder if perhaps most or even all the other galley slaves might be liberated. But the Brotherhood of Diablo had responded too quickly. In any case, their auxiliary fleet would never sail from Colinga Harbor tonight. Nor would they be in condition to organize any kind of naval pursuit for many days to come. And the scattering of his guerilla bands would make even land pursuit difficult.

"That's the last of 'em, Derek!" cried someone behind him.

Dragging their heavy chains to the bow, the galley slaves tumbled over the side; the water was only a few feet deep here, and they were able to pull themselves along the lines rigged to shore. When the last of them were gone, Derek waded to the stern and vaulted into the water. He swam the width of the channel and clambered up onto the rocky strand.

The longboats were not far behind; he could see the grotesque hulking forms of the Rathugs silhouetted against the inferno that only an hour ago had been Colinga Harbor. Running, leaping, scrambling, sliding, he rounded the steep promontory on the side facing the sea; then he was on the flat shingle, and he raced headlong through the night.

Not a single one of his own men was still in sight;

even the grove of dwarf oaks seemed deserted. But then he saw two big green lights gliding toward him out of the darkness.

"Our men were here and gone about ten minutes ago," Willie reported. "Then you started moving the other way, and I almost went with them." He grinned impudently. "Looks like a big bonfire."

At that moment the whole grove turned as bright as day. They were startled; Buck's hackles rose and he growled sullenly. It was the gasoline storage-tanks exploding—a very big bonfire indeed.

Chapter 5: The Battle of the New Sea

"There she goes!" a man cried in Rollo's ear, almost causing him to drop the tray he was carrying toward the chart-house at the stern of the ship. "That means we fight!"

Far away to the south, across the phosphorescent waters of the New Sea, a pillar of fire lighted the sky. Rollo became aware of the combined fleets of the Wise Woman and the Fisherfolk riding at anchor all around him; over a hundred swift galleys armed with rams, their reinforced metal prows projecting just under the water. Then somebody boxed his ears.

"This should teach me a lesson!" growled his father. "I let you talk me into coming, and now you just stand around gawking like an idiot."

Rollo hurried off with his tray. He had indeed

promised to make himself useful if they let him come along tonight, even volunteering to help the cook down in the galley. His father had been against it at first, but his mother had helped talk him into it. He just hoped that his father didn't think he had been sent as a spy.

He heard a clicking sound from the platform near the top of the mast, and signal lights began to flash all over the fleet. The corps of signal-girls had been organized by his father; they did most of their training at night, and his mother always seemed to find excuses to go down to the docks and look around. The shipwrights often laughed about it on the job.

Not that Rollo blamed his father; the women were always wriggling their hind ends at him when they walked past. He just wondered sometimes how many half-brothers and -sisters he had growing up around him.

He delivered the food at the chart-house door and hurried back to the galley with his empty tray. The pillar of fire to the south had already lost its first explosive flare, and now burned with a steady orange-red glow. Then he realized that one of the ships was moving slowly toward them across the bows of the fleet, and he dived behind the forward hatch and silently watched it approach.

What little breeze there was came out of the west; the sea was calm, and its warm saline waters lapped softly against the side of the ship. Bright splashes of stars spangled the moonless sky. The red and gold sails of the ships all around him had been furled; the rowers sat expectantly at their benches.

The oars of the approaching ship were banked as it came alongside; then a gangplank was thrown out. Rollo could not recognize any of the men crossing in the darkness, but the figures of Eva and his old tormentor Jana were unmistakable. He already knew that Eva held supreme command, so the ship that had just pulled alongside was probably the flagship of the entire fleet, the men its leading captains.

All eyes watched them as they moved toward the stern. Certainly nobody watched Rollo. It was no problem at all to slip unseen the entire length of the ship, swing over the rail, and work his way hand over hand around to the rear of the chart-house. The stern porthole stood wide open for ventilation, and he braced himself against the taffrail and peeked inside.

Margo lounged on her fur-covered divan; her face was painted exotically, and she wore a long silken robe of green. Books, charts, and various brittle old maps lay scattered about her. She may have been disappointed that Eva had been given the supreme command of the combined fleets, but her exotic paint only made her look intense and raptorial, not envious.

It was Rollo himself who was the most disappointed. Eva now wore a plain blue shirt and dungarees, and he recalled with boyish fascination how she used to look with hardly any clothes on at all. Jana wore the same costume, scaled down to her own diminutive size. He sometimes wondered why she never grew any bigger.

The captains who entered the chart-house with them represented the two fleets about equally. Margo harangued them at length, although none seemed quite sure what she was talking about. Eva, on the other hand, came straight to the issue, going over their plan of battle point by point.

Rollo did not really understand what she was talking about either—"sheering," "envelopment," "holding the center," and so forth—but the captains nodded, and for once even Margo had nothing to say. Then he noticed Jana suddenly raise her head and look in his general direction. He ducked.

Through the opening just above him he could hear Eva continuing to address the war council, her words half muffled by the rhythmic lapping of the sea against the ship, the creak and groan of its timbers as it rolled gently in the water. The orange-red glow to the south was still bright; it was after midnight now, and the moonless sky was as dark as ever. Cautiously he started to raise his head.

The next thing he knew a hock-like arm shot through the porthole, grabbed him by the scruff of the neck, and yanked him like a surprised kitten into the chart-house. Then he was soundly boxed on the ears, and even these grim men laughed. But the worst thing of all was that Eva should see him treated like this, and he flushed with embarrassment, unable to meet her eyes.

"Sit in the corner over there," his father growled. "One peep out of you and I'll throw you overboard."

Rubbing the back of his neck, he did what he was told. It was obvious that Jana had accidently spotted him and told his father. He glared at her. But she only smirked and wriggled her eyebrows.

The conference continued as if he were merely part of the furniture. Then the two signal-girls were summoned and given messages for the rest of the fleet. Rollo noticed that his father seemed unusually gruff with them, and that there was a twinkle in Jana's eyes as she watched.

A brief discussion about cannon and grappling hooks followed, and Eva pointed out the importance of the sun being in the enemy's eyes.

At last the conference broke up and the grim-faced captains began to file out the door. Rollo, still feeling humiliated and ignored, raised his head. Eva turned and looked at him for a moment, then disappeared through the door. And although Rollo himself one day became a mighty man of the sea, whose name was celebrated throughout the rediscovered lands of the earth, he never forgot that look. For in it lay the secret of all glory and adventure.

Jana awoke with the feeling that she was being smothered. The steady, rhythmic splash of the oars had lulled her to sleep, but the oars were silent now; the ship lay becalmed in the water, and the consciousness of hordes of people—including Rathugs—oppressed her from all sides. She yawned and stretched and knuckled her sleepy eyes.

Then she saw Eva standing at the rail nearby. It was beginning to dawn, but the dim gray light was at Eva's back; whatever interested her lay to the west.

Jana rose and stretched again; as her senses awakened she realized that there were more Rathugs nearby than she had thought. All to the west. She hurried to the rail, and Eva lifted her up so that she could see better. But for several minutes she could only gape in astonishment.

It was the most incredible thing she had ever seen in her life. She could just make out the dim shorelines on either side of the Great Channel; but the towers of glass and metal that rose out of the sea all around them glistened luminously with the reflected light of dawn. Many of the towers had been battered down by storm-waves; but where their hulks acted as breakwaters, the towers behind them rose unscathed hundreds of feet into the sky. Some appeared to be made entirely of glass.

Their flagship stood at the very center of the Great Channel, but Jana could not tell how far the line of ships stretched on either side of them. The line of monstrous black hulks facing them seemed to stretch from shore to shore, and she remembered something that Eva had said at the war council last night about forcing the enemy to extend his line as far as possible. And they were still extending it; moving their ponderous galleys up and back, trying clumsily to straighten their confused formation into some kind of order. They had come to punish fleeing slaves, not to be challenged in battle. Even Jana could see that they were unprepared.

Then Eva had to put her down. Now that it was morning the signal-girls had replaced their lantern devices with colored flags. Eva called one of the girls to her and gave her a message. A few moments later flags were waggling back and forth down the entire line of ships.

It didn't mean anything to Jana—the signal-girls were Gunnar's business—and she looked for something to stand on. But the moment she turned around she was blinded by the angle of the sun, which meant that the Rathugs facing them would be blinded too—at least for a while. She remembered Eva talking about that at last night's war council as well. She dragged a bucket to the rail and jumped up on it.

Just then she saw a puff of smoke from one of the enemy ships; an instant later a concussion wave almost knocked her down. The cannons! But no sooner had she steadied herself than their own ship suddenly jolted forward. She grabbed the railing with both hands. They were attacking the enemy! But only half their line—every other ship.

More puffs of smoke. Concussion waves buffeted her back and forth. Something whooshed past the bow. Then she realized with horror that they were heading straight at a monstrous galley over twice their own size. This time the smoke and concussion wave came at almost the same instant, as the enemy vessel bore down on them. Fortunately the cannons of the Brotherhood of Diablo didn't seem very accurate. Maybe because they had the sun in their eyes.

Then Eva was beside her again, holding her tight. They were going to collide! But at the last instant she heard the captain shout something behind them. Their ship veered suddenly to starboard, and the rowers on the port side banked their oars. A horrible, tortured sound of snapping wood resounded between the passing ships, and splinters clattered on deck all about them.

Jana glanced back. All the oars on one side of the enemy galley had sheered away, and it was turning slowly in a circle, while the Rathugs on deck screamed orders and ran wildly back and forth. At that instant a ship from their second attacking line rammed the crippled galley at full speed. Backing water, it left a gaping hole in its side.

Eva held her tight as their own ship turned and shot back through a gap in the enemy line. No wonder she had wanted them stretched out! Their own small ships were much faster, and could now shoot in and out of the gaps. Crippled galleys were being rammed left and right. The Brotherhood of Diablo could no longer fire their cannons without endangering their own ships.

Then they were turning again; once more the blinding sun was at their backs. Eva signaled the slingers and pikemen to take their battle stations; this time they were not aiming merely to cripple an enemy ship. In fact, the monstrous black galley was already too crippled to maneuver in the water—but not too crippled to sail back to Diablo. It was even now unfurling its black sails.

This was the flagship of the Brotherhood of Diablo, preparing to sail for home. The trap was unsprung; the auxiliary fleet that should have enveloped the enemy from behind hours ago was still nowhere in sight. But the Rathagon would not rest until he was avenged. Next time they would have more and better cannon; more boats with motors; an invincible fleet. Then would this day's humiliation indeed be remembered!

But Eva's flagship was still very maneuverable, and it bore down on the monstrous galley at ramming speed. Eva braced herself, holding Jana tight. But the collision still almost pitched them both overboard. There was a lull; then both flagships exploded into noise and fury. A barrage of pikes and sling-stones screened their own rowers as they heaved and heaved at their oars.

At first nothing happened; their beaked prow remained imbedded in the side of the enemy flagship. Then slowly—grinding, splintering, groaning—they began to back water.

"Look at the hole!" cried Jana. "They won't get very far—" Then she remembered that the Brotherhood of Diablo chained their galley slaves to the oars, and fell silent.

At that instant Eva dived headlong to the deck, turning so that she would not land on little Jana. The huge iron grappling hook bit into the bulwarks right where they had been standing. With a jolt their ship came to a halt. When Jana looked up she saw that several more grappling hooks had bitten into the ship's bow, that they were being drawn back slowly toward the monstrous black galley, and that a line of hulking Rathugs was preparing to board them.

Now they were the ones who were helpless in the water. The Rathugs hurled their javelins with terrible accuracy; few of the slingers were still on their feet, many of the pikemen were down, and several rowers lay pinned to their benches like insects. Closer and closer they were drawn toward the monstrous black galley.

"Axes!" cried Eva, scrambling to her feet. "Hack away the grappling lines!" She left Jana sheltered behind the rear mast with one of the signal-girls, then raced back to the bow and began sawing at a grappling line with her knife.

Jana realized that the little signal-girl crouching next to her was even more frightened than she was, which encouraged her. The girl clasped the crucifix around her neck and prayed fervently for both of them.

When Jana at last peeked out she saw that Eva had begun to rally the crew; most of the grappling lines had been hacked away from the bow, and the surviving rowers again heaved at their oars. But still the line of hulking Rathugs glowered down at them, ready to board them the instant the two ships came close enough. Not twenty feet separated them.

Suddenly Jana realized that one of these Rathugs was strangely familiar. His helmet covered most of his face, but she was certain that she knew him from somewhere although it was hard to concentrate with so much noise and confusion, with so many people crowded all around her. Then she had other things to worry about.

The oars on the far side of the enemy galley were still intact, and the monstrous black hulk began slowly to veer broadside. The grappling lines could now be hurled from stem to stern, and the barrage of missiles became even more devastating.

But Eva was prepared for just such a tactic, and the lines were immediately hacked away. It was now more difficult to maneuver, however; and the rowers on the side facing the enemy ship had to fend it off with their oars. Eva got her surviving pikemen and slingers arranged in a shield wall; but the murderous javelins of the Rathugs were still taking their toll.

Then Jana realized that for some reason the stern of their ship, where she huddled with the little signal-girl, was drawing closer and closer to the enemy even though the grappling lines had apparently all been hacked away. She looked up and saw three hulking Rathugs pulling on a taut line. She jumped up and peered over the stern.

An iron grappling hook lay snarled in the rudder chains. But as she turned and started to shout a warning she was hit with a blinding flash of light, as if the sun had suddenly reversed directions. Then she realized that they were drifting toward one of the glass towers, the sun reflected directly into her eyes, a blinding pillar of light hundreds of feet high.

At last she began to shout; but her shrill little voice hardly carried ten feet through the din of battle. She could see that the Rathug flagship was sinking—but not fast enough. If they could capture the galley that she was on they might still save themselves, perhaps even return to battle. Jana snatched up the knife of a dead pikeman and went to do battle on her own.

Crawling down into the rudder chains she took the knife in both hands and began sawing at the grappling line with all her might. She had actually cut through several strands when something caused her to look up—just in time. The javelin skimmed right over her neck as she dived forward.

Snatching and scrambling, she tried to regain her balance, but the weakened grappling line could no longer hold the strain of two tugging ships. It snapped into the air, writhing and uncoiling like a wounded serpent, and Jana was knocked from the rudder chains.

She hit the water flat on her belly. Stunned, she sank like a rock. Too shy to let people see her undressed, all that she knew about swimming was from watching Derek and Eva. She kicked and squirmed, and somehow managed to get her head out of the water for a moment. But there was nothing to grab hold of, and she coughed and gasped for breath.

When she tried shouting for help, she only got another mouthful of water and found herself sinking again.

But no matter how hard she kicked and squirmed this time, she just could not seem to reach the surface. Her lungs were in agony; she could hardly keep herself from breathing water. She felt tired, very tired; so tired that it seemed pointless to struggle any more. Then something had her by the hair, and she shot to the surface like a cork.

Blind, coughing and sputtering, all she knew was that she was still alive, that somebody was holding her head above the water. Then she felt herself being towed backwards. Whoever it was, they seemed to be alone in the water; her own ship was a good fifty yards off, and pulling away fast. She sensed Rathugs somewhere nearby, but she could not see their flagship anywhere. Had it already sunk? She was afraid that if she turned around and looked she would only get another mouthful of water.

Then she found herself beside a jagged wooden plank; instinctively she clutched for it, and the person who had been towing her hoisted her out of the water to perch atop it. She winced as a sliver stung her hand. Pulling it out with her teeth, she looked around.

"You saved our ship," said Eva, treading water beside her. "I didn't see that grappling line until it knocked you overboard."

"But where's our ship going?" cried Jana, trying to find a more comfortable way of straddling the rough plank. The water was much colder here than on the other side of the New Sea, and she shivered.

"I'm afraid that they didn't see either of us go overboard, and none of the other ships seem to be heading this way. We've won the battle, but it looks like we now have some swimming to do. Hold tight a minute!" And she let herself sink underwater.

Then Jana became aware of a commotion not far away, and she turned around just in time to see the monstrous black flagship roll onto its side like a dying whale. Slowly it sank beneath the surface. Leaping, scrambling, plunging into the sea, the surviving Rathugs grabbed frantically for any flotsam within reach. She tilted her little head to one side in concentration.

"It is him!" she cried. "I thought there was somebody familiar aboard that ship."

At that moment Eva surfaced again. She had stripped off her boots and clothing, keeping only her belt with its knife and scabbard.

"There's Fatty," said Jana. "You remember, that big ugly hulk who came to Saluston and got the Gunks to . . . Oh, oh, I think he sees me."

Clinging to a spar and paddling clumsily toward them like some fleshy sea-monster, the Rathug looked even more menacing now than he had in the dim corridors of Saluston. He glared balefully at Jana. There was no doubt that he recognized her too.

For just a moment she was apprehensive. But then Eva began towing the plank backwards, easily outswimming the clumsy paddling of the Rathug. Could he really swim at all? He still clung anxiously to his spar, holding his shaven, fleshy, bejewelled head awkwardly high out of the water. Jana stuck out her tongue at him and impudently waved goodbye.

He bellowed with rage and churned the water to foam in his clumsy efforts to overtake them, but Jana only laughed merrily and began making faces at him.

Then all at once she sensed something above her, and turned around so fast that she nearly capsized the plank. The glass tower loomed hundreds of feet into the air; waves washed in and out of it at sea level and some of its windows were broken for three storys above, but the rest seemed liveable.

"Oh, Eva!" she cried. "I never thought to check—"

But Eva's naked body slipped silently beneath the water and was gone. Now Jana became apprehensive again; very apprehensive. The Rathug, still clumsily thrashing and kicking and clinging to his wooden spar, was now less than twenty yards away. And she was alone. And he was getting closer.

She tried paddling backwards; but then stopped. If she got any closer to the glass tower a wave might catch her and smash her to pieces against it.

She peered anxiously down into the gray-green water, but could not see very far below the surface. She certainly could not see Eva. What was she doing? Whatever it was, Jana hoped that she would stop doing it soon and come back. Fatty was getting too close.

Then he suddenly bellowed in pain, and began to claw and stab furiously at something beneath him in the water. His violent churning again turned the water to foam, but the foam was no longer white. A red stain began to spread outward over the surface. He bellowed and whirled around, trying futilely to stab whatever had just hit him from behind.

Then the wooden spar which he had been clinging to was mysteriously jerked away and sent skimming out of reach. A moment later Jana saw Eva rise to the surface, take a deep breath, and disappear again. But it was behind the floundering Rathug, and he still had no idea where she was—until her knife plunged into his side.

The red stain had now almost reached Jana. Attacked again and again from below, the Rathug still kicked and thrashed at the water—but it was obvious that even his inhuman strength was rapidly seeping away. The weight of his boots and armor dragged him down, and there was nothing that he could cling to anymore. His cries grew weaker and weaker. Until at last, still thrashing feebly, he slipped forever beneath the sea.

Jana gave one firm nod. ''Serves you right, Fatty!''

Then Eva rose out of the water beside her. There was a hard glitter in her eyes like that which Derek sometimes had after a battle, and it made Jana uncomfortable. But not as uncomfortable as the rough plank that she was still straddling, or her wet clothes, or the chilly water.

"Hold very tight and don't move," cried Eva. "There may still be some jagged glass around that opening."

Garlands of slimy maroon seaweed draped most of the lower storys of the tower like rotted curtains. They could not see very much inside, but they were in the middle of the Great Channel, and the closest ship was now about two miles away. The waves, rebounding from the colossal structure, made any approach rough and treacherous.

"Oh, Eva, I've got to tell you—"

"Tell me when we're inside!" she cried. "Here we go!"

Riding the crest of a wave, they swept through the maroon curtain of seaweed. Then they were scrambling over more seaweed, rotted carpeting, jetsam, and weathered tile and concrete. Jana got water in her nose and began to cough violently. But Eva never let go of her.

At last they found themselves on a dim staircase. There was a door in front of them, which seemed to have been recently painted. Eva now wore only a belt and scabbard around her waist; her naked body glistened with seawater, and her hair fell in a mass of wet coils around her bare shoulders. She tested the door.

It seemed to be in good repair, and she pushed it open and stepped inside.

"Now will you listen?" cried Jana, hurrying after her. "When I checked before the battle, I never thought to check above me. There are people here, Eva. Lots of people."

Chapter 6: Breakout

"But you can't even find a Mog without me," Willie protested. "Not until you actually see one, at least. Then it's too late." He added frimly, "I'm staying."

Derek had expected retaliation after the burning of Colinga Harbor; but it looked now as if the Rathagon had mobilized the entire Brotherhood of Diablo in pursuit—even part of his bodyguard of Mogs. Derek had to admit that they would have been trapped a dozen times already except for Willie. But now they really were trapped, completely.

Willie continued, "What would Jana think of me if I ran out on my friends when things got tough?"

"They're more than just tough, I'm afraid. But you're quite sure that Jana is somewhere to the west of Diablo? There seem to be only small islands in that direction.''

''Whatever is there, that's where she is.''

''But not above us anymore?''

Willie laughed merrily. ''You still don't believe me, do you?''

''Yes, I believe you,'' Derek said thoughtfully. ''Somehow Jana and Eva must have ended up at the top of one of those glass towers. Why, I can't even imagine. They won the battle.''

''Destroyed their whole fleet,'' Willie added. ''I wish we could have stayed to watch the end of the fight, but I never thought the Rathugs would be after us so soon.''

''Neither did I. But you still haven't been able to find Eva again?''

Willie shook his head. ''As I told you, she and Jana were somewhere above us. And then all those smelly trucks came bouncing and roaring up the coast, and we had to run for it. And they kept after us for days. Then Jana started moving west.''

''And Eva?''

''I couldn't find her anymore. But really, Derek, I think we're just too far away.''

''Even that night when you and I and Buck slipped back to the northern coast?''

''She was gone,'' he admitted reluctantly. ''Otherwise we were close enough. . . .'' He shrugged. ''She didn't go west with Jana. Maybe she went in another direction.''

Neither mentioned the obvious alternative. The sultry breeze wafting in over the cold offshore currents meant that it would probably be another foggy night. That was one thing in their favor, perhaps the only thing. For the last three weeks the cordon had grown tighter and tighter, and now there was no place left to run. The scout ship of the Brotherhood of Diablo, which they had surprised one night as it lay at anchor, was barely large enough to transport the sick and wounded off the island.

"I said I'm staying, and I mean it." Willie folded his arms and stuck out his little chin.

"Well, then we'd better get the ship launched before dark. Or it's sure to end up on a rock somewhere."

He left Willie sitting with Buck beside the stream, and hurried off through the darkening willow grove to order the launching. There had been no cowardly panic to rush aboard this last ship from Diablo. Those left behind knew that they were now penned into a blind corner of the island, that a wall had been thrown up across the only pass, that Mogs had been loosed against them; but they were more desperate for vengeance than to merely save their own lives.

"Anyone from the Fisherfolk will see that this is delivered." Derek handed the sealed packet to the captain. Even if he himself did not survive, all that he had learned about the island's defenses, about the Rath of Diablo itself, would find its way to Eva . . . or to somebody who could use the information. And in case they did break out, he also indicated an inaccessible stretch of the northern coast where Jana and Willie might safely be brought close enough to talk. "It's too late to reach the Great Channel before dark. Just get away from these treacherous waters and ride out the night at sea. Good luck!"

Derek watched the black ship pick its way through the maze of rock and shoals until it had safely reached open water. He had given them more food than he could really spare; with all the slaves liberated from Colinga Harbor, there were now hundreds of men and women penned together here.

But food was not their most urgent problem—it was escape. Tomorrow would surely see the Rathagon's final act of retaliation. He summoned his captains to the willow grove for a last council.

"When attacked—attack," he exclaimed. "When you have no choice but to fight, never wait for the enemy to come and get you. Get him first. Questions?"

The discussion lasted until dusk. Fog was beginning to roll in by the time Derek rejoined Willie and Buck. It would be a dark, chilly, desperate night, and they shared the last of their food beside the stream.

Willie said, "The last time I talked with Jana, she said that this Margo was a cold-blooded stinker. She must be, if it was her idea about how to silence Rathug sentries."

"I'm not proud of it either." Derek sighed. "But it's saved our lives already several times, and I can't think of any other way of dealing with the sentries. At least, not silently."

"But do you think it will work with Mogs too? They really are awful, you know." He shuddered. "Even to think about."

"Then let's not think about them—until we have to. Ready?"

No Mog had ever been killed in battle; they had already taken an awful toll of his men. Storming the wall thrown across the only pass out of this corner of the island was their last desperate chance, and it had to be done tonight. But a single Mog on the loose would make such an attempt mere suicide—and there were a full score of Mogs encamped with the Rathagon's army at the head of the pass. Margo's technique had worked well against Rathug sentries. Would it work against Mogs?

He had once tried concentrating the fire of all his slingers on one of them. They had not really injured the mindless brute, but it had been driven berserk, and started killing its own men. The Rathugs had at last brought it down with a technique of their own. Which of the two techniques his men would use tonight would depend on the positions of the Mogs themselves.

He divided the bulk of his forces into two arms that would sweep outward and reconverge at the pass—behind the enemy encampment. All the trucks were apparently on this side of the wall. And all the Mogs. Some of the men that he kept with him carried heavy pole-axes; others carried metal barrels filled with bottles of gasoline. Even the barrels themselves would serve a purpose.

"A guard," said Willie. "Just on the other side of those bushes."

Derek waved his men back and slipped the hatchet from his belt. Sheer weight was the greatest problem with Margo's technique. Some Rathugs weighed over four hundred pounds. Keeping to the low-lying ground where the fog was thickest, he crept silently forward.

But this particular Rathug weighed barely three hundred pounds. Nor was he very alert. The last thing that the Brotherhood of Diablo expected was for the vermin they had penned up here to attack them. Nonetheless the guard did wear a helmet, which meant Margo's cold-blooded technique was perhaps the only way he could be killed in silence.

Derek waited until he was a few steps past him, then sprang silently out of the fog, sweeping his hatchet in a low plane. It severed the guard's spinal column at the base of his back, killing him instantly. Derek braced himself to catch the huge trunk as it folded over the lower half of its body, so that no heavy clattering fall would attract attention.

Willie was at his side before he had even wrestled the dead weight to the ground. He whispered anxiously, "One of the Mogs woke up a couple of minutes ago and left the encampment area."

Derek hesitated; this was something completely unexpected. Where was the Mog going? In their own mindless way, Mogs delighted in all manner of foulness; no obscenity or act of viciousness was beyond them. Nor could they be underestimated. They had a brute's mentality, but also a brute's cunning. Had this creature heard something and cunningly hidden itself in the fog? Or maybe it was just answering a call of nature?

"No, it's still moving down the valley," said Willie. "It's up to something nasty."

"We can't go back now," Derek said at last. "They'd only come for us tomorrow or the next day. Let's go!"

Despite the rolling fog, they could smell the Mogs before they reached their tents. There were no guards here. Who would dare approach a Mog at any time of day or night? The tents stood at the very edge of the encampment, alone and downwind, where their bestial foulness was not so oppressive to the rest of the army.

Derek led the way forward. Not one of his men hesitated. Then they were in the tents and their heavy pole-axes crashed down on the skulls or spinal cords of the sleeping Mogs. The stench became overpowering as the sphincter muscles of the dead giants collapsed. Derek stumbled back into the open air. One by one the others appeared.

Willie remained silent for several moments. "Got

'em all,'' he whispered at last. ''Except the one that left.''

''Where is it now?''

''About half a mile that way. Maybe we'll be gone by the time it gets back.''

''Just stay with Buck—and try to keep him out of the fight. Where are the others?''

After a moment: ''In position, on either side of the pass. Oh, let me give the signal!'' He tried to whistle, but his mouth was too dry. ''I'm still scared,'' he muttered, after making some ineffectual hissing sounds. At last he let out a shrill whistle.

The night erupted in noise and confusion. The tents of the dead Mogs were doused with gasoline and ignited; flame and explosion penetrated the fog from the direction of the parked trucks; men beat the metal barrels with axe-handles, raising a hollow racket that could be heard for miles. It awakened the entire camp.

Willie ran over and helped beat one of the metal barrels, grinning delightedly at the noise; but Derek snatched him up and set him on Buck's back. Everything thus far had gone according to plan—almost. Somewhere out in the mist there was still a Mog on the loose.

''Here they come!'' cried Willie.

Derek turned and signaled to his men. Every Rathug in the encampment was now coming straight toward the source of noise and commotion—and away from the wall blocking the pass. It had to be overrun quickly, or they would never break out at all. Derek led the way as they circled the camp; Buck ran noiselessly along, with Willie clinging to his back.

Nature had had little to do with the construction of the pass. A precataclysmic road had been cut through the mountains; just a routine job for the lost skills and machines of the people who had once lived here. The Rathugs, on the other hand, had had to marshal a whole regiment of slaves merely to throw up a single crude wall. A good twenty feet high, with a watch-tower at one end, it stood at the very crown of the pass.

The fog was not as dense here, and torches burned all along the top of the wall. The Rathugs could see their attackers clearly. Very clearly. Several had already been killed by the time Derek arrived.

But if the attackers could be seen clearly, so could the defenders. Some men and women had managed to scramble over the wall in the first surge; but their rope ladders and grappling hooks were even now being hacked away.

"Slingers!" cried Derek. "Follow me!"

A makeshift wooden stairway ran up one end of the wall to the watchtower, but it was so narrow that a single Rathug could hold back an army—if he could hold his position. The barrage of slingstones cleared all defenders from the stairway. Derek himself led the charge to the top.

One of the Rathugs, torn and bleeding from the slingstones, had retreated into the watchtower itself.

He was an enormous hulk covered with greasy red hair like some kind of primitive ape. He reappeared the moment the barrage ceased. But he was groggy and slow, no match for the furious speed of Derek the Hunter.

Then the entire wall was cleared, and hundreds of men and women were scrambling up the stairway, over grappling lines and rope ladders, to safety on the other side. Derek was so busy organizing his rearguard and insuring that none of the wounded was left behind, that he never heard the shrill little voice calling frantically to him from below.

Willie had sensed the Mog coming toward them just as Derek led the charge up the stairway. He yelled and yelled; but there was so much noise that nobody heard him—except, perhaps, the Mog itself. Then he began having trouble with Buck. The great beast's perceptions were nowhere near as keen as his own, but the Mog was very close now. Its stink penetrated even the dense fog.

Then it came lurching into the torchlight. Nine and a half feet high, thickly covered with dark, evil-smelling hair, it was easily twice the weight of even the most hulking Rathug. There was no controlling Buck anymore; Willie slid from his back and ran for cover.

Buck leaped at the monster's throat—and was knocked sprawling like a puppy. Willie peeked out from behind a rock; he hadn't been seen, but he certainly would be the moment he tried to reach the wall. It was Buck that he was most concerned about at the moment, however. The great beast was not used to being knocked about like a puppy. The Mog had not even broken stride.

Then there was a panic among those still waiting to climb over the wall. The Mog was coming right at them, and now there were sounds of the main force of Rathugs returning to their encampment.

Buck had not been hurt—except his pride. He hit the back of the giant's leg with a rending, clawing fury that sent it reeling. Not even the gristly flesh of a Mog could withstand such razor claws, such powerful jaws and teeth.

This was Willie's chance—and he took it. Dodging from rock to rock, he scampered for the stairway. A hundred Rathugs would come charging out of the fog any minute now, and he wanted to be on the other side of the wall when they did.

But then Buck was knocked sprawling again, and once more Willie was forced to dive for cover. Terribly clawed, bleeding from a dozen gaping wounds, the berserk Mog had now lost all control over its inhuman strength. Screaming with pain and fury, it raged back and forth, dismembering the bodies of attackers and defenders alike. It snatched up a dead Rathug like a doll and tore it to pieces. Willie ducked as the stump of a huge leg sailed past him.

What was he going to do now? The Rathugs were almost on top of him; but the minute he came out of hiding he would have his arms and legs torn out of their sockets and the rest of him squashed like a bug.

"No, Buck! No!" came Derek's voice.

Willie peeked out. Buck was on his feet, badly mauled and limping, but ready to attack again. This was the only time that Willie had ever seen him hesitate to obey Derek's command. But Derek himself did not hesitate. He hurled a pole-axe into the face of the mindless brute and leapt out of reach.

"Willie! Buck! Over the wall!" he cried, as the monster lurched after him, tearing the axe-blade out of its crushed jaw.

But Derek made no attempt to escape the screaming, raging horror; he seemed to be deliberately taunting it from just out of reach. Then it charged after him, and he turned and plunged into the rolling mists, staying just within sight until he heard the oncoming Rathugs just ahead. Then he put on a burst of speed, cut at right angles from the line of pursuit, and circled back.

The wounded monster lurched straight into the line of Rathugs, and its rage and fury drove them back with terrible slaughter.

Meanwhile Willie had at last reached the stairway; but Buck refused to follow him. Growling and limping back and forth, he seemed tempted to go off into the fog after Derek. His huge green eyes had never shone more brightly, but the fog was too heavy, the night too dark. He could see nothing.

"Oh, please, Buck!" Willie coaxed him. "Climb

the stairs with me. Derek will be all right if we just—''

At that moment Derek himself came leaping out of the fog. ''Let's go! Over the wall!''

Willie was surprised to find some men with pole-axes waiting at the top of the wooden stairway. But he kept moving—over the top and down the other side.

''Cut it away!'' cried Derek, and the men began chopping at the supporting beams of the stairway. There would be no immediate pursuit.

Derek quickly examined Buck. He seemed to have been only badly mauled and bruised, but he limped painfully. Derek himself carried Willie this time, and they hurried down the old roadway toward the northern coast, a good three days march away. Buck hobbled silently along beside them.

Chapter 7: The Floaters

Jana doubted that she would ever make a very good sailor; the voyage had barely begun—they had not even reached the choppy waters of the Great Channel—and she already had nothing left in her stomach but dry heaves. Vertiginous gray-green waves rolled and swelled beneath the fleet little galley, which seemed to pop up and down like a giddy cork. She groaned and headed for the railing again. At the moment she really did not care if one of the black patrol ships did catch them.

Nor was there anybody to comfort her. She still had no idea what had become of Eva, and had already forgotten half the questions and nearly all the information that she was supposed to communicate on this mission. And why had Derek chosen so remote a corner of northern Diablo? She had heard the sailors on board complaining that the whole stretch of coast there was almost inaccessible, that it would take some very tricky seamanship to get even close enough for her and Willie to talk. They were still muttering about the direction of the wind and the peculiar surge of the waves, and especially about the dark sullen clouds that obscured the sun. For some reason they avoided the open sea, hugging unusually close to shore—as it turned out, dangerously close.

Spindrift pattered her brow refreshingly, and she opened her eyes and raised her face from the rail. The galley was at last nearing the Great Channel, and far down the coast she could see the big glass tower where she and Eva had found themselves after the sea-battle. It looked so flimsy at this distance that she still wondered why it had never toppled.

The old Professor, who seemed to be in charge of the strange castle where the people in the glass tower had sent her, had explained to her all about "earthquake construction"—which, as far as she could understand, had something to do with triangles (whatever they were)—and was always ready to answer any questions she had about almost anything at all. Not even Margo knew so much about so many different things.

"Please try to eat some biscuits, Jana," said a shy and gentle voice behind her. "If you had some food in your stomach, I believe you would feel better."

Jana merely groaned, without even opening her eyes.

Marie was the Professor's granddaughter; a frail and timid girl of seventeen, whose hair and skin were both as white as the marble statues that surrounded the pool at the strange castle where she lived with her grandfather. She was so shy that she blushed whenever anybody spoke to her, and especially at any mention of Derek the Hunter.

She spent nearly all her waking hours reading books, although not the big thick volumes read by her grandfather or little Margo. Only after patient and affectionate coaxing had she revealed any part of her private world of glorious fantasy. A world of noble adventure, handsome princes and beautiful princesses, of ogres and dwarves and witches, of hobbits and evil necromancers. But her most glorious fantasy of all was now Derek the Hunter, and she knew that he was one of Jana's friends on Diablo. Her firmness in persuading her grandfather to allow her to accompany him on this voyage had surprised everyone—perhaps even Marie herself.

"Please try, Jana," she said. "Just half a biscuit."

Jana did try, and succeeded. But then she made the mistake of staring at the choppy gray-green waves rolling all around her—and was right back where she started. For a moment she felt like just throwing herself overboard.

But she knew that her mission today was too important, that she was now the official Communications Officer of the whole rebellion against the Brotherhood of Diablo, and that its success or failure might depend on the questions and information she had been sent to transmit to Willie. Even if she did not much feel like eating biscuits just now, she was very happy that Marie had come along—to remind her what the questions and information were. She laid her little face on the cold wet railing and groaned.

Then all at once she was jolted back into alertness, literally jolted. There was a sickening lurch, and a shudder passed through the entire ship. A moment later they were once more popping up and down on the gray-green waves like a giddy cork, but sailors were now shouting and running toward the bow, and some of the rowers were leaving their benches. She glanced up in wonder at Marie.

The frail young girl, with her marmoreal white hair and skin, appeared spectral in the overcast sullenness of the day; she also appeared confused by what had happened, although not at all afraid. That was left to Jana—who was afraid enough for both of them. Not even the billowing volumes of water that she saw outside the ship had distressed her like the tiny trickle that she now saw inside it.

Standing on her tiptoes, she peered over the rail at what lay behind them. She could just discern a shadow beneath the water: they must have scraped the roof of a submerged building of some kind.

Fortunately they were within a few miles of the entrance to the Great Channel, where they could tie up in safety at one of the glass towers while they made repairs.

Jana helped with the bailing, and although the water she dumped over the side hardly balanced the spindrift blowing in, the work at least gave her an appetite, and she managed to keep down two whole biscuits and a hardboiled egg. The ship did not appear badly damaged, and she only heard some muttering about the "keel" and "sluggish handling." She also gathered that the ship might be too slow to outrun one of the black patrol ships.

Then they were in the choppy waters of the Great Channel. Strangely enough she began to feel better—especially when she saw a glass tower looming dead ahead. She had no idea how long the repairs would take, and hoped that Derek and Willie would not become too impatient. The northern coast of Diablo sounded like a miserable place to keep people waiting.

She was alert enough now to resume checking for danger. The glass tower they were beating toward seemed vacant of all but some primitive and insignificant forms of animal life. The waters around it also seemed vacant. Then she began searching in other directions, for she had heard that the black patrol ships were more active than ever since the Battle of the New Sea.

She gasped. "Marie, where's the captain? I have to . . . There he is!" And she scurried the length of the ship to the bow, where emergency repairs were proceeding under the captain's personal supervision.

He was perhaps the only man on board who really understood her presence on this voyage, and the real nature of its mission. Not even emergency repairs distracted him from giving her his full attention. Nor did he for an instant doubt her warning.

"Hard to starboard!" he cried, and raced to take the helm himself.

The crew were so surprised by the order that they were at first slow to respond, but at last the crippled galley began to veer out of the Great Channel toward the open sea. Perhaps the crew's obvious reluctance to sail in that direction, under today's peculiar wind and wave conditions, also had something to do with their slow response. Even under the captain's experienced touch the ship handled sluggishly.

Then they saw it, and cries of alarm ran up and down the benches of the rowers, spurring them to redouble their efforts, as one of the mates began to beat the tempo. The black patrol ship was probably returning from a reconnaissance mission among the islands of the Fisherfolk—following the New Sea coast of the archipelago, while they themselves had been hugging the ocean side. Except for Jana's warning, the two ships would have entered the Great Channel within a mile of each other.

The black patrol ship immediately veered in pursuit, but merely as a gesture of supremacy; it had no real hope of overtaking one of the fleet little galleys of the Fisherfolk. But the distance between the two vessels did not widen; if anything, the ponderous hulk of the Brotherhood of Diablo actually seemed to be closing in. Then the race was on.

At first Jana did not understand the desperation with which her own ship tried again and again to force its way back to the coast only to be anticipated and cut off each time by the pursuing galley. Surely such experienced seamen could not be afraid of the open sea. The wind and wave conditions were indeed rather peculiar, and the sun was utterly blotted out by the brooding clouds, but surely this was nothing that the Fisherfolk had not seen before.

Or perhaps it was because they had seen just these conditions before. Jana herself began to sense their desperation, as they plowed the gray-green billows, mile after mile, straight out to sea. The captain had now relinquished the helm, and was again supervising the emergency repairs. Still, the hulking black patrol ship continued to close. Ordinarily, after making a gesture, it would have abandoned its pursuit by now; but it had sensed something unusually sluggish about its prey, and its banks of oars beat the water with a rhythmic fury. It was close enough now so that the cracking of whips could be heard.

"Look, Jana," cried Marie, "the sea all around us seems to be blossoming. Are they flowers? I've never seen any plants bloom so fast."

"You still haven't," said Jana. "Whatever they are, they're not plants. There are thousands of them!"

As if by some conscious purpose the strange blossoms seemed to be massing upwind of both galleys; as their pinkish-white heads expanded it could be seen that they were really a kind of irregular sack, some now larger than a man, swelling rapidly.

"What are they, captain?" cried Jana.

"Floaters!"

But he had no time to explain, and ran from bench to bench, pulling certain select men from their oars. The galley was now barely moving in the water, and nobody seemed to care that widening trickles were again pouring through the damaged bow. The black patrol ship had closed to within a hundred yards.

Jana was not surprised to see the men that the captain had pulled from their oars arming themselves with slings. What was surprising was to see them forming ranks at the bow, instead of facing the enemy at the stern. Then she realized that one of the floaters had swelled into a hug bag nearly half the size of the ship—and was beginning to rise out of the water!

Up and up it went, trailing behind it thin tentacles hundreds of feet long; it was drifting straight toward them. The captain shouted orders, and they sluggishly began to pull to starboard—but not quite fast enough. At another order the men at the bow commenced firing slingstones at it. Jana was certain that she saw at least five direct hits, but at first these seemed to have no effect.

Then she saw that the floater was slowly contracting and losing altitude, and at last drifted harmlessly by the port side only a few feet above the water, dragging its long tentacles behind it. But now there were several more floaters rising slowly into the air, and the sea for hundreds of yards around was blossoming furiously with pinkish-white gasbags. The hulking black galley of the Brotherhood of Diablo now stood dead in the water, uncertain which way to turn.

But Jana knew. She at last understood what was going on, and ran to the captain, pointing to what looked like the very densest mass of swelling gasbags. Once more he accepted her guidance without hesitation, resuming the helm himself and barking encouragement to his rowers.

A few of the slingers resumed their oars; but it was now a sargasso of draggling tentacles, and the ship seemed only to inch its way straight toward the very heart of the deadly sea. The remaining slingers at the bow continued to hurl their missiles with furious accuracy, and there was a faint smell of gas in the air. Then there was a cry from the bow, and one of the repairmen limped backward and collapsed, holding his left leg as if it had suddenly become paralyzed.

"Oh, some of the tentacles are slipping through the hole in the bow!" cried Marie.

Jana realized the danger but could only nod her head dizzily as the smell of gas in the air grew stronger. Several floaters had deflated in the vicinity of the ship already; now the air was filled with them. She began to stagger drunkenly toward the rail, a silly grin on her face, but Marie grabbed her and hugged her protectively.

Then Jana heard dizzy cries of joy, although she had not the vaguest notion why everybody was so happy.

"Take a deep breath, dear," she heard Marie's voice, as if at a great distance. "That's right. Now another deep breath."

Jana's head at last began to clear, and as she looked around she realized that there were no more floaters in the air—at least, in front of them. But she counted nine of them hovering directly over the black patrol ship, as if anchored to something on deck; they were slowly descending their own tentacles toward whatever was in their grasp.

Once more she started to move toward the rail, in order to get a better look. This time it was the captain himself who stopped her.

"Don't either of you move until we've cleaned the sides."

There were only a few men at the oars now, merely to keep the ship headed into the wind; the rest were working very diligently (and very gingerly) to scrape away every broken strand of tentacle from every part of the vessel. The bow was the first to be scraped clean. Then the emergency repairs were resumed.

The first thing Jana noticed, when she was finally permitted to go to the rail, were the houses. The water beneath them was now so shallow that the remnants of a precataclysmic island could be discerned even through the gray-green billows. Perhaps that explained why there were no floaters in this particular direction.

But for whatever reason, the captain lost no time picking his way over the submerged island and circling the colony of floaters. With the full crew at the oars, and the wind at their backs, the galley achieved better than half its original fleetness on the return voyage, reaching the Great Channel by late afternoon. But they were still not yet fast enough to outrun the black patrol ships.

It was not one of the glass towers at which they now tied up for repairs; at least, there was no glass remaining. A skeleton of rusty girders, with crumbling sections of brick wall clinging here and there like rags of decaying flesh, loomed into the murkiness of late afternoon.

But a scavenging party discovered enough material for adequate repairs, although divers reported that the damage to the keel could not be mended without more equipment. They pushed off just after dark at what the captain estimated was a good three-quarters of their regular speed—a safe margin for outrunning any patrol ship they might encounter.

If the voyage had been unlucky so far, they were now more fortunate as they approached the remote corner of northern Diablo; only the gruesome western coast of the island was more treacherous to navigate. The cloud cover began to break up, and the moonlight filtering through was enough to reveal the necessary landmarks for bringing the vessel close to shore, where great rolling storm-waves drove a pounding surf against a wall of sheer cliffs.

Jana still did not remember all the questions and information that she had been sent out to convey; but Marie sat beside her, shielded by the bulwarks, with a dark lantern and a specially prepared logbook. In the glimmer of light the girl's frailness and white hair made her seem more spectral than ever. But she waited patiently; so patiently in fact that she began to wonder if they might have to bring the ship closer to shore after all.

Then Jana suddenly burst out laughing. "Willie was asleep, and was grumpy at first about our coming so late. But now he's wide awake—I think he was very worried that something might have happened to us—and just went to wake Derek." She did not notice how the mere mention of the name affected the girl sitting beside her.

The roar of the breakers was frighteningly close; perhaps only the captain himself really understood why the ship had to battle the heavy swell, threatening at any moment to dash them to splinters, through the middle of the night. No anchor could have held them, and the oarsmen had to row twenty miles just to keep the ship in place.

Traps and breakouts, armies marching, smelly trucks, Rathugs and giants chasing them, raids, fires, battles lost and won; Jana related every last event of Willie's account—all dutifully recorded in the logbook by Marie, along with Derek's replies to several important questions of strategy. Not that Jana really understood what it was all about; but as official Communications Officer she did her job without too much reasoning why.

She beamed. "Derek just sent me his compliments through Willie. He says that I've never been so accurate and efficient. Should I tell him about you, Marie?"

"Oh, please don't say anything to him about me," the girl whispered, as if afraid Derek might hear her from a cliff over a mile away, through a roaring surf. "Don't, please don't!" Her eyes blinked rapidly, on the verge of panic.

"All right," said Jana with a complacent nod. She was not at all unhappy to have gained a new reputation for accuracy and efficiency (something that she had certainly never enjoyed before). "Nothing else to communicate?" Then she was silent for several minutes, her little head tilted slightly to one side; her strange gamut of facial expressions were like those of someone daydreaming.

The cloud cover had scattered completely and the wind had veered a full ninety degrees by the time they at last pulled away from the coast. But they were no longer fortunate in having so much moonlight, for they were spotted by another hulking black patrol ship that chased them for several miles before giving up.

It was just after dawn that they began beating their way across the choppy waters of the Great Channel, and the whole ship bobbed dizzyingly in the gray-green waves. Jana once more stood at the rail, her eyes closed and her face pattered with spindrift, groaning in misery.

"Please try another biscuit, dear," Marie said gently. "I'm sure you would feel better."

Chapter 8: Castle Island

Jana felt much better this morning now that she was a comfortable distance from the sea. After sleeping most of the previous day, she had just finished her second breakfast and was already thinking about dinner. But she was not allowed to forget her ghastly voyage to Diablo.

As she gazed down from the castle window into the garden below, she noticed Marie and a tall woman in a white smock helping a man toward a bench. The man limped painfully on his left leg, but at least he was able to walk. Jana recognized him as the member of the repair crew who had been paralyzed when some floater tentacles slipped through the damaged bow of their galley. She was glad now that she had been too exhausted last night even to dream, for she had no doubt that it would only have been a nightmare about floaters.

The garden itself must once have been a paradise of bowers, arbors, and splendid marble terraces, although its grounds were now planted with only neat rows of vegetables. Beyond it the waters of a colossal marble swimming pool shimmered in the morning sunlight. But nobody swam in it anymore; it was stocked with fish which two attendants in white smocks were feeding with table scraps at the very moment. Nothing was wasted here, but none of the splendid marble statues of naked men and women, toppled during the cataclysm, had ever been replaced on their pedestals. Some ornamental pillars also lay toppled near the swimming pool.

But not everything had toppled. She recalled what the Professor had told her about "earthquake construction," and how the big glass tower where she and Eva had found themselves after the sea-battle had not toppled like so many other things. But she had not yet learned what had become of Eva. . . .

"Good morning, Jana," said a voice behind her. "Are you feeling better?"

"Oh, hello, Marie. Much better, thanks. I saw you down in the garden. Is that sailor's leg going to heal?"

"Grandfather says that the poison will wear off in another day or two." Her timid blush lent her a touch of color, or she would have been as white as the marble statues toppled around the pool below. "He's ready for you now."

Jana slipped down from the windowsill and affectionately took her hand. She knew that real people were sometimes vague and shadowy to Marie, that she had a continual tendency to retreat into her own private world of fantasy and that, after their voyage to Diablo, Derek the Hunter had become more glorious to her than ever. A tinge of pink touched her marble-white skin as she listened to Jana relate an anecdote about him from their days at Saluston.

Every corridor they passed through, every hall and room along the way, was arrayed with art treasures from many lands and times: magnificent paintings and statuary, priceless furniture, brilliant carpets, tapestries, and mosaics. Unlike the statues and ornamental pillars outside, these had all been restored after the cataclysm; the damage to the castle itself had been slight and long since repaired. There were other gardens than the one beneath Jana's window; some of these were used to nurture plant species that had not existed until recently anywhere in the world.

Marie had explained how it had all been assembled years before the cataclysm by an "eccentric millionaire" —which was about as clear to Jana as "earthquake construction." But there was no doubt that it was all very beautiful.

Margo, on the other hand, only found it very useful. The people who lived here now—they called themselves *scientists*—had spent decades salvaging books from around the New Sea and beyond. Margo had moved into the vast library, and was in the process of reading it from end to end. She had brought old Clara Johnson with her, and put her to work as a librarian. For some reason this seemed to amuse Margo. It was the closest that anybody had ever seen her come to a smile.

Jana and the girl tiptoed past the library door. Margo was never very genial company, and the old hag made their skin crawl. Embrasured windows looked down on a garden of exotic flowers, most of which had not existed before the cataclysm. But poor Marie could not appreciate them. Her pinkish eyes were very weak, and she was almost devoid of any sense of smell. They crossed the magnificent entrance hall and turned down a long corridor lined on both sides with statuary.

"Poor grandfather!" sighed Marie. "He's always been so proud of his skill at chess . . ."

"Until he taught the game to Margo?"

The girl nodded sadly. "It was so embarrassing for him."

"Yes, Margo's always been very good at traps and surprises. Cold-blooded stinker!" she muttered.

They found the old man hunched over a chessboard with a book of chess problems in his hand. Jana had also learned the game, but so far she hadn't found anybody that she could beat.

"Good morning, Professor," she said innocently. "Are you practicing for your next game with Margo?"

He laughed good-naturedly. "Yes, it was rather humiliating. After all these years to have a little girl annihilate me hardly ten minutes after I had taught her the game." He scratched his long white hair in perplexity. "Then I set up five classic problems on five separate boards, and she solved them all in less than a minute."

"Are you giving her intelligence tests too?" asked Jana.

"I tried, but it was no use. The test turned out to be only mechanical—how fast could she write the answers? Neither I nor any of my colleagues has yet discovered a means of interpreting the results. I'm afraid that we will still have no satisfactory method of measuring her intelligence."

"She's got a big brain, huh?"

"Well, her cranial index is somewhat larger than normal. But it's more than just a matter of brain size. You see, my dear, even the brightest people use no more than ten percent of their brain in thinking. Margo evidently uses a much higher percentage. Perhaps even different parts of her brain."

"Different parts? I thought it was all one brain."

"The human brain is really a composite of several evolutionary brains, one enfolding the other. At the very center is a kind of crocodile brain."

"That solves the problem," said Jana. "Margo's using her crocodile brain. By the way, how did I come out on the tests?"

"You have, uh, shall we say, unexceptional intelligence."

"Is that a polite way of saying I'm a dummy?"

"Not at all, my dear. Your intelligence is in fact somewhat above average. It's just that your brain seems to be constructed in an unusual fashion. At least, as far as we can determine from standard tests. The only real way to find out, of course, is to open up your head and take a peek."

Jana looked alarmed, but the old man only laughed and patted her hand.

"I'm just teasing, my dear. What is really intriguing is that there is another being like yourself. Now if the two of you should be capable of reproduction," he muttered to himself, unaware that Jana was blushing to her ears. "Why, it might lead to the creation of a new species. Or, at least, a new variety. I'm still not completely sure of the difference."

"There's a big difference in the world, isn't there, Professor?" asked Jana, trying to change an embarrassing subject. "Everything changed almost overnight, they say."

"Well, not quite that fast, my dear. Nature seldom does change very fast—it only seems to, sometimes. It used to be called the Pendleton Effect, but I'm sure you aren't—"

"What was that name?" Jana cried excitedly.

"Pendleton, Dr. Derek Pendleton. Sometime before the cataclysm—"

"That's *his* name too—Derek the Hunter."

"Oh, I see." The old man smiled indulgently. Like many people he tended to forget that Jana was not just the dainty little girl she appeared to be. "But the name really wasn't that uncommon in the old days. There were hundreds of Dereks, maybe thousands. You have no idea how many people there used to be then, my dear."

"No, Professor," Jana insisted. "Derek Pendleton. That's the name of Derek the Hunter—as well as his grandfather, the Founder." And she tried to recall everything that she had ever heard about the founding of Saluston. This was not really a great deal, and she was much more informative about the Gunks and how the Brotherhood of Diablo had organized their revolt. She also mentioned the machines—although she still didn't know much about them.

But the Professor did. Every scientist at the castle knew about the machines being gathered by the Brotherhood of Diablo and how they would probably be used. Their defenses secured them against the galleys of raiders, but not against a great armada equipped with cannons and propelled by motors. The Battle of the New Sea had given them an unexpected respite.

"I've often wondered about what became of old Pendleton." He removed his thick spectacles and wiped them thoughtfully on the tail of his shirt.

"He was a professor too," said Jana. "Like you are."

"Well, uh, thank you, my dear. But my title is just, shall we say, honorary. Pendleton was a real scientist, one of the greatest of his day. I've been able to trace most of his career through his books and articles—until just a few years before the cataclysm. Then he just seemed to vanish. I've never discovered any notice of his death, although I must admit that my records are incomplete.'' There was a wry look on his face. ''So that's what happened to him.''

''Grandfather,'' Marie said timidly, blushing with shyness. ''What about Lester? He's been in there a long time now.''

''Oh, my goodness! I forgot all about him!'' He turned to Jana. ''This is your last test, my dear. That's why I asked you to come here this morning. Now tell me if you can. Where's Lester?''

''I've been wondering about that myself,'' said Jana. ''He seems to be right here in this room, and at the same time very far away.''

''Ah, but where in this room?''

She pointed to a tall metal cabinet surrounded by storage batteries and cables.

''Very clever, my dear,'' said the Professor. ''But he wasn't as easy for you to find as usual?''

She shook her head. ''It's like he's at the bottom of a mountain. He's usually very easy to find, this close,'' she added dryly. ''What's the test all about anyway?''

''Well, we've all been curious about how your extraordinary powers of perception—''

''May I let him out, Grandfather?'' said Marie.

''What? Oh, yes, of course. In fact I'll do it

myself.'' He unhooked the cables and opened the cabinet doors. ''I'm sorry to have kept you locked up so long, my boy.''

''That's all r-right, Professor,'' said Stinky, emerging amidst a waft of gaminess. ''Anything for science.'' He grinned awkwardly at Marie, who blushed. ''Something I c-can run and get for you? I'm fast, you know.''

''That you are, my boy,'' said the Professor. ''According to my tests, you may be the fastest two-legged runner ever to live on earth.''

Stinky glanced complacently at Marie, as if he already knew about her infatuation with heroic deeds and attributes.

''Now why don't you two go out into the garden,'' the Professor suggested. ''Thank you for your help, Lester.''

''Any t-time at all, Professor. Mighty p-p-pretty flowers out in the garden, Marie.''

''Too bad she can't smell them,'' said Jana when they were gone. ''Or maybe it's lucky.'' And she burst into merry laughter. ''But how come Stinky seemed so far away when he was inside that cabinet?''

''Well, we've wondered if you were somehow able to detect the electrical impulses of the brain at great distances. So I created an energy field around this metal cabinet to block those coming from the subject inside. We seem to be on the right track.'' He nodded thoughtfully. ''Although none of us suspected that your extraordinary powers of perception were quite so, well, so perceptive."

"They're not so perceptive when I'm seasick," said Jana. "I just wish I would have known about Derek's grandfather before we sailed for Diablo. He's always been interested in why Saluston was founded, and about the cataclysm, and things like that."

"Well, surely he's read his grandfather's books?"

Jana shook her head. "They were probably thrown into the Abyss with the others. Derek only had the library of a professor of literature. Novels and stories and such. Margo always sniffs at them."

"Well, I've always enjoyed novels and stories, no matter what Margo thinks. Read everything I could get my hands on, in fact."

They sat comfortably on a bench just outside the door. It was a pleasant summer day, and the pitcher of cold fruit punch on the table before them was already beginning to sweat. The gangling Newcome lad with the little round head gallantly attended the frail, dreamy girl with snow-white hair through the flower garden below.

Jana waited with patient curiosity; she knew that the Professor's story would be interesting.

Chapter 9: The Pendleton Effect

The Professor thoughtfully wiped his spectacles again although they were already perfectly clean.

"I was just about Margo's age when the cataclysm began," he said. "The scoutmaster and all my friends were killed in one of the landslides, but all I got were some scratches and bruises. No broken bones. For days and days everything kept rocking and swaying up in the mountains; then a new wave of explosions started—probably the last attack of the war—and I could see the great tsunamis, hundreds of feet high, come rolling in over the cities below. Then just when things began to settle down a bit, the whole coast started to drift northward and the Central Valley was completely inundated."

"Were you by yourself?" asked Jana.

"Yes, but I had been on boyscout camping trips before, so I knew how to take care of myself. Food was no problem, even for years afterwards. There were heaps of canned goods everywhere I went, and a few people survived here and there, and some of them helped me. But the only real friends that I had were books. Then one day I realized that these books could never be replaced. I had collected stamps as a boy, but now I started collecting books. I already had a growing library when I first made contact with the Fisherfolk."

"Did you live here in this castle then?" asked Jana, pouring them each a cup of cold fruit punch.

"No, that was much later. I lived with the Fisherfolk for some years, collecting old books and works of art wherever I could find them. And people—I soon discovered that I wasn't the only one still interested in such things. Then I heard reports about this castle, and I came here and found it deserted and not too badly damaged. Although you can see that we still haven't quite put everything back in place yet. It had been a millionaire's toy, and it already had a large library of its own. So my colleagues and I shipped our collections here, and we've gone on collecting ever since."

"Weren't you bothered by the Brotherhood of Diablo?"

"This castle is a real castle, my dear. Besides, we're on a stormy island, and the Brotherhood of Diablo have always been clumsy sailors. At least, until lately. Nor did they have cannons then to knock down our walls."

"They wouldn't need cannons to break the glass on that big tower out in the Great Channel. Why are your people there?"

"It's our observation post, my dear. With our telescopes we can see almost everything that happens on Diablo. Except for the Rath of Diablo itself, unfortunately."

"Too much fog?"

"Well, there's certainly enough fog. But in this case the mountains block our view. According to the old maps the Rath of Diablo stands on the site of the region's largest maximum-security prison. In fact, it may be the identical structure. We don't know much about it. I had hoped to question some of the prisoners after the Battle of the New Sea. . . ." He shrugged.

"But no prisoners?"

He shook his head. "It was Margo's opinion that she already had sufficient data concerning Diablo, so prisoners were of no further use to her. Then she said something about half measures inevitably leading to ruin."

"Cold-blooded stinker!" Jana muttered. "But what about this island, Professor? You say that the Fisherfolk brought you here?"

"Ah, yes, the Fisherfolk. Ironic that those at sea had a better chance of surviving than those on land. The fishing fleets hardly noticed the tsunamis that rose as high as mountains wherever they reached land, or the earth movements that shifted crustal plates a hundred miles. This wasn't an island then, by the way."

"Yes, Derek told me that even the New Sea used to be dry land. But why did you say that everything didn't really change overnight? It sounds to me like it did."

"The effects did happen very fast indeed, but only after the causes that produced them, growing in force every year, had reached a critical threshold. That's the Pendleton Effect I was telling you about. Let me give you an example from right around the corner. There used to be a structure not too many miles from here called the San Andreas Fault, where two plates of the earth's crust slowly slipped past each other. But it was never a steady event. That is to say, the force driving the plates was steady, but there was no actual movement until a certain threshold was reached, until the driving force had grown to a point where it overcame the friction resisting it. Then everything seemed to happen at once."

"Earthquakes," said Jana, helping herself to more fruit punch.

"Yes, but rather weak compared to the tectonic movements that created the New Sea."

"Then this Pendleton Effect has to do with earthquakes and things like that?"

"In a way, but also with living things. Let me give you another example. Long, long ago the earth was ruled by giant reptiles called dinosaurs. They flourished for millions and millions of years in a tropical environment near the equator. But very slowly the continents drifted into colder latitudes. Meanwhile new plants and animals were evolving, perhaps the number of the dinosaurs themselves dwindled slowly toward a critical minimum. Then all at once—geologically speaking, at least—they became extinct. Although the forces leading to the extinction threshold had actually been building up for millions of years.''

''Is that what happened with the cataclysm? Forces slowly built up—then bang? Why didn't somebody say something?''

''Many people did, but those in power could always point out that there was no real evidence of harmful effects. None that were obvious to the voters and taxpayers, at least. So they just kept poisoning the land and water and air with all kinds of chemicals, and these kept recombining with each other in unexpected ways. Half the countries in the world had atomic weapons by then, mostly just as a matter of national prestige. Nuclear power plants were everywhere, and their radioactive wastes were disposed of very haphazardly.''

''I know about bombs. Margo says that the old Wise Woman told her about big underwater explosions off the former seacoast.''

''Why, that's exactly what I and the rest of my boyscout troop were watching when the landslide hit us. Way out at sea we could see what looked like gigantic white domes rising out of the water. I remember how angry our scoutmaster was. 'They've finally done it!' he cried. Then he started cursing, with tears running down his face.That's all I remember until I found myself lying at the bottom of a pile of debris with two dead boys on top of me. But I still remember the controversy,'' he added. ''It was in all the newspapers and even on television.''

''About the bombs?'' asked Jana, who was not quite sure what he was referring to now.

''Well, that too, of course. The superpowers were all piling up arsenals of atomic bombs, deploying them all over the planet, and getting more and more nervous about who would be the first to pull the trigger.''

''Who did?''

''Well, if Dr. Pendleton was right, it may have been the planet itself. But let me get back to the controversy I was telling you about. Somebody came up with the idea of dropping the canisters of radioactive wastes into a submarine canyon off the coast. The old coast, that is. Well, these canisters kept piling up—there were evidently underwater currents that nobody had properly explored—and some of the canisters may have been smashed. Then some scientists began to warn the government that, no matter how far apart these canisters were dumped, the underwater currents were sweeping them together into a kind of atomic pile—in several parts of the submarine canyon, if I remember correctly. In any case, there was the growing fear that an enemy might somehow bring these piles to critical mass.''

''What's that?''

He looked doubtfully at her for a moment, and scratched his shaggy white hair. ''You see, energy equals mass times the speed of light squared. Which means, well. . . .'' He looked doubtfully at her again.

''Never mind, Professor,'' said Jana. ''Just tell the story. You gave me an intelligence test, so you know I'm a dummy about such things. Are you saying that these atomic canisters you were talking about were turned into atomic bombs?''

''Ah, that's very clever, my dear. It may indeed be best to, well, to omit the more technical details.'' He wiped his perfectly clean spectacles again. ''The real gist of the controversy was that this submarine canyon was part of a fault line where two crustal plates met. And what evidently happened was just what the scientists said would happen. One underwater explosion was somehow triggered, then another; and then one plate started sliding over the other. Or something like that. There was no more controversy after it happened—or newspapers or television sets for that matter. The war lasted only a few days.''

''Who won?'' asked Jana.

''Nobody. There were only losers.''

''Then this was the trigger you were talking about? And Derek's grandfather gave the warning that nobody would listen to?''

''No, no, my dear. It was something entirely

different. In fact, he wrote a whole book about it. Evidently just before he built this underground refuge in the mountains, which you and your friends left some time ago."

"We didn't exactly leave," said Jana. "We were chased out by Gunks and agents of the Brotherhood of Diablo. But most of what Derek's grandfather and the other professors built was already wrecked. They threw their books into the Abyss."

"A great loss, a very great loss indeed." The old man sighed. "Whole libraries of books lost forever."

They were silent for several minutes. The Professor looked sad as he thought of so many books now beyond any hope of being collected. Jana still looked perplexed about many of the things she had just heard.

She frowned. "I think I understand why the world is all changed. But why are people and animals and plants so much different now?"

"Oh, dear. I'm afraid that's rather complicated."

"You don't have to give me any details," said Jana. "I probably wouldn't understand them anyway. I just want to know why people are so much different now. Me, for instance."

"Well, there was once a man named Darwin, and he made a famous theory that all species had evolved from lower forms of life. He believed that chance individuals were born with some peculiar trait that gave them an advantage in competition with others of their kind. That is, they were better adapted to their particular environment, and thus tended to survive longer and produce more offspring. Most of these offspring also carried the favorable trait, so it became more and more common each generation. On the other hand, those members of the species that lacked this environmental advantage tended to be selected against, and to leave fewer offspring. Do you understand?''

Jana nodded slowly. ''Like the people of the old Wise Woman having long legs because the slave raiders caught all the slow runners?''

''Hmmmmm. Well, perhaps something like that. Although I doubt if Darwin believed that natural selection would operate so fast. Which, of course, is one of the problems with the whole theory.''

''You mean that maybe species didn't evolve from lower forms of life?''

''No, they evolved all right, including human beings. Exactly how they did it, is the problem. You see, there is no clear evidence that a single species ever evolved out of another through natural selection. Darwin thought the process might take several hundred thousand years.''

''I don't think it took that long,'' said Jana. ''At least, not this time.''

''Maybe never,'' the Professor added thoughtfully. ''It's hard to imagine any environment so static that a new characteristic would be a continual advantage for so long a period of time. Besides, natural selection is merely a kind of passive reaction, whereas life itself is active and dynamic." He shrugged. "I really don't know. But I suspect that sudden mutation, perhaps as a result of some intense environmental stress, is the real cause of new species arising. Although natural selection is certainly a factor in determining which new species survive. But even natural selection itself may not be so passive as it appears. Perhaps the brain perceives an environmental need and somehow influences the body's genetic code. I'm just guessing now, of course," he added. "What's wrong, my dear?"

She frowned. "I'm trying to remember something Derek once told me about mutation. I think he said that the cataclysm threw all of nature into a mutation panic. Something like that, anyhow. But I think he was referring only to those who were outside Saluston when it happened." She added, "Both my parents were outside, I think."

"What were they like?"

"My parents?" She shrugged. "I must have been very young when they died. I've always been pretty much on my own—at least, until Derek took me in. But I don't think the Newcomes that I told you about were changed in any way. As far as I know, they weren't any different from the Founders. Although their children were much different. Like me."

"But they were changed, you see. There are billions of cells in our bodies, each with its own particular shape and function. These cells are continually dividing into new cells that are exactly like themselves.

Special chains of atoms form codes for them to follow, and when an organism reproduces itself similar chains of atoms from each parent combine and determine what the offspring will be like. Not exactly like its parents, but usually very similar. Unless the genetic code is somehow disturbed. This happens all the time in nature."

"You mean that these special chains of things get broken up, and the offspring has, let's say, only one ear, or its foot where its head should be?"

He laughed. "No, no, my dear. Genetic changes don't affect just one part in isolation from all the rest. A famous scientist named Cuvier said: 'Every living organism forms a complete entity, and no part can change without changing the other parts.' That's called the Law of Correlation."

Jana thought for a minute. "That's like the cataclysm then, isn't it? I mean, the whole world was like a single living organism, and as soon as one part was changed, all the other parts had to change too."

"Well, it seems I may have to re-evaluate your intelligence test after all," he said, and they both laughed. "But, of course, all mutations imply the simultaneous mutation of many characteristics at once. And as for the chains of atoms I told you about getting broken up, that really isn't necessary to create wholesale genetic changes. All that really has to be changed is the regulation of how the genes act upon each other in the timing and duration of their effects. Particles called enzymes do the regulation."

"So if these enzymes are changed a little, then the creature may be changed a lot—even if his gene things aren't much changed?"

"I'll make a scientist out of you yet, my dear," and they both laughed again.

Jana sipped her cold fruit punch, and gazed thoughtfully down at the garden of strange flowers, where two strange young people strolled through the warming sunshine. She did not really understand much of what the Professor was talking about, although she had a personal interest in the subject. Nobody like her or Willie had existed before the cataclysm, and nobody like them existed anywhere else in the world even now.

"Then these changes in living things could happen even without a cataclysm?" she asked.

"They happen all the time. In fact, in the years just before the cataclysm, men had learned how to make them happen. It became fashionable among biologists to experiment in genetic engineering, despite a lot of protests. There were safeguards set up to reassure the protesters—strict regulations, watchdog committees, rigid inspections, expensive decontamination systems, and so forth. But such safeguards always depend upon the peaceful continuity of maintenance. Once that breaks down . . ." He shrugged. "How many of these experiments broke loose during the cataclysm, or how they affected people and animals and plants, we'll probably never know. As far as I can determine, there was a big research center of that kind on what is now Diablo. It was called the Directed Evolution Project.''

''Sounds spooky,'' said Jana.

He nodded ruefully. ''There were a lot of spooky projects in those days. People were not only experimenting on how to fight each other with bigger bombs, but with smaller and more lethal germs. Uncontrollable diseases must have killed millions and millions of the people lucky enough to survive the bombs, and even when the germs didn't kill them right away, they changed their genetic structures so that their children and grandchildren suffered instead.''

''Spookier and spookier,'' Jana muttered. ''And all these things happened at once?''

''And more. No event on earth happens in isolation from the rest of the planet. Any event that upsets the balance of nature also upsets everything in nature that depends on that balance. And not just here on earth, my dear. There also seems to have been a brief blast of radiation from outer space. Although that was one aspect of the cataclysm of which man was innocent.''

''Blast of radiation?'' she sighed. ''Don't bother to give me any more intelligence tests, Professor. You're making me feel dumber by the minute.''

''I'm sorry, my dear. It is rather complex, and I don't really understand a lot of it myself. But tiny particles are constantly showering the earth from all directions of space, and these in themselves can cause genetic changes.''

"But that must have been happening before the cataclysm?" said Jana.

"Not really to any great extent. You see, the earth's magnetic field acts like an umbrella against these showers of radiation."

"Are you saying that the cataclysm wrecked that too?"

"No, no, the destructive powers of mankind are fortunately not that vast." He frowned thoughtfully for several moments. "Yes, I'm sure that Dr. Pendleton and his colleagues must have built Saluston for exactly that reason. In his last book he warned about the imminent collapse and reversal of the earth's magnetic field. Now although this seems to be a regular phenomenon in nature—"

"The trigger!" cried Jana. "That's the trigger you were talking about, isn't it?"

He nodded slowly. "Why, I believe that's just what it was. The whole world had been brought to a critical threshold, just waiting for the right trigger to nudge it across. It turned out to be a collapse of the earth's magnetic field, although it might have been almost anything—human error, faulty equipment, terrorism, political upheaval, even mere time."

"Time?"

"Exploding population and the rampant pollution of the environment with insidious poisons and chemicals were also nearing a critical threshold. Many parts of the world were growing desperate, and not much more time would have been needed for any one of them to have acted as the trigger.''

Jana nodded. ''There were dead zones everywhere, caused by poisons and chemicals. I told you about them. They must have killed lots of people and animals. No plants grew in them.''

''They were probably a factor in this mutation panic too. The pollution of the environment was probably creating genetic stress even before the cataclysm. There were safety systems here too, but these became more and more complex, and hence more susceptible to human error—especially those safeguarding nuclear power plants. And then there were warning systems; all over the planet nervous men sat with their eyes on a radar screen and their thumb on a button. Then a natural phenomenon pushed the button for them, and bombs and missiles started flying, safety systems started breaking down. I suppose it was a kind of environmental chain reaction. In any case, it didn't all happen at once, my dear. It only seemed to.''

''The Pendleton Effect,'' said Jana. ''But what about the Brotherhood of Diablo? They're all mutations, aren't they? They're all ugly and nasty enough.''

''There are all kinds of mutations,'' he said thoughtfully. ''Most are indeed degenerative, and hence have little chance of surviving in competition with creatures refined by many generations of natural selection. Nature isn't very bright, although tenacious and immensely powerful. Under environmental stress, she just starts throwing off mutations, in hopes that at least some of them will thrive under the new conditions. There may even be social mutations. The Brotherhood of Diablo seems to have thrived by turning the conventions of siege or famine into an institutionalized economy. Terrible people, really terrible!"

Jana was silent for several moments; when she spoke at last it was as if to herself. "Then if a new creature never meets another of its own kind, they just die out without leaving offspring."

"Did you say something, my dear?"

"Uh, here comes Margo, and she's got . . ." She was silent for a moment. "Yes, it's Korso. He must have just returned from taking Derek's letter to the Fisherfolk." She laughed merrily. "He's been getting so fat lately! They didn't feed him very well as a slave, so now he's making up for it."

"There you are," said Margo from the doorway. The fantastic beauty of the garden below did not seem to affect her in any way. "Come, we must be aboard ship within the hour."

Jana groaned. "Oh, I just got over being seasick!"

Meanwhile Korso had summoned Stinky in from the garden; Marie came with him.

"I'm off to w-war," he said. "And I won't c-c-come back unless as a hero, so you can be p-proud of me."

Marie whispered, "I wish you'd take the awful old woman with you. She makes everybody's skin crawl."

''Old Creepy. Don't let her w-worry you none. Just keep your b-back to the wall and watch what you eat.''

Margo seemed even colder than usual. She had a message from the Council of the Fisherfolk in her hand, and its contents evidently did not please her.

''It seems that I am again relegated to the role of insuring that any military advantages that may accrue are not dissipated through predilections of dogmatic humanitarianism.''

''Is that Derek's plan?'' asked Jana. ''The one he sent in the letter?''

''As modified by the sounder strategic capacity of our Supreme Commander. Derek's heroism and prowess in the field are unimpugnable.'' She sniffed. ''But he reads novels.''

Chapter 10: The Giant Killer

One after the other the swift little galleys shot back out through the narrow entrance of Colinga Harbor. The work begun by Derek the Hunter was now complete. Every ship in the harbor was ablaze; powder magazines exploded one by one, scattering the ponderous warships and their cannons across the waters. The last remaining fleet of the Brotherhood of Diablo would never sail again.

"That was easy," said Jana, standing on a bucket at the rail. On the mast above her flew the pennon of the Supreme Commander. "I thought we were in for a fight."

"We are," said Eva. "But this fleet won't be part of it. The Brotherhood of Diablo isn't used to people fighting back. Half their strength lies in sapping the will to resist.''

''I'm glad they won't have any more cannons.'' She peered across the blazing harbor. ''I think those ruins over there . . . or maybe those over there . . .'' She shook her head. ''Willie said that he and Derek burned all their shops and foundries where they made the cannons.''

Eva smiled. ''Well, the next time you get close enough, you can tell Willie that you and I burned their fleet to the water.''

Jana glanced up at her, and they both laughed. ''I just hope we don't end up in the water ourselves, like the last time.''

She remembered how surprised they had been to find people in the tower of glass. But there was nowhere else they could go; they were out in the Great Channel, and their closest ship was miles away. Eva found dry clothes for them—the glass tower had evidently been some kind of residential building before the cataclysm—and they went exploring. This was very tiresome, because the people in the building were all near the top, hundreds of feet above.

She climbed and climbed, until at last she just sat down and cried with weariness. Then Eva picked her up and carried her the rest of the way—forty-seven flights of stairs, she counted. It took them hours to reach the top; several times they left the stairwell to look out of windows. It was terrifying to be so high in the air. Jana had the giddy feeling that any minute the glass tower was going to keel over and carry them with it back into the sea.

They were able to catch the people unaware. After one glance Eva slipped her knife back into its scabbard. There were twelve men and fourteen women; none of them looked very robust, and most wore thick spectacles. If she and Eva were surprised to find people here, the people were astounded to find them.

But they were all civilized, in a nervous, ungainly sort of way; the men were especially nervous when they talked to Eva. They had witnessed the Battle of the New Sea, and were now even more astounded to discover that Eva herself had been the Supreme Commander. Then they let Jana look through a telescope, and the next day she had her first ride in an elevator—and her last until the day she left.

For what she saw through the telescope was their flagship and five other galleys returning to search for them. Eva sailed off with them the very next day, and soon afterwards Jana herself was on her way to Castle Island, then a coasting voyage to Diablo, and the misery of seasickness. . . .

Eva turned and signaled to the captain of her flagship; they were the last to leave Colinga Harbor, and the crew pulled at their oars with a will. Jana held tight to the rail as they shot through the narrow channel. Dawn was just breaking over the mountains across the New Sea, rose-violet above jagged, contorted ramparts of deep purple. The sea itself spread before them like a sheet of warped glass.

As the sun rose in the sky the gray-green waters slowly brightened into turquoise; there were few clouds and almost no wind. Jana was glad that it was such a calm day, because she had had a big breakfast. But she knew that this calm would not last much longer. She could see the smoke screen billowing from rows of smudge-pots in front of the beach just ahead, and she knew that the Brotherhood of Diablo was marching this way.

The battle would probably be decided before noon—one way or the other.

"Can you find any of these Mogs yet?" asked Eva, as their fleet of swift galleys moved through the flotilla of heavy transports anchored just offshore.

Jana shook her head. "They're still too far away to be sure. Even Willie is so far away that I can hardly find him. Or maybe it's because of those black mountains in the way. This really is an awful place."

"I'm glad you can find Willie at all," said Eva. "No matter how far away. But I don't think we can expect any help from them today."

"They'd help us if they could," said Jana. "But Willie said that they're being chased all over the island, and that they would have been caught a dozen times at least if he hadn't warned them."

"Our invasion may take some of the pressure off them—at least, for a while. But I don't see any way right now of getting you and Willie close enough to talk."

"Didn't Derek say in his letter that he'd try and send scouts? Maybe we can give them a message?"

"Could you distinguish his scouts from, say, the slaves of the Brotherhood of Diablo?"

She shook her head.

The few cannons salvaged by the Brotherhood of Diablo were ineffectual; the smoke screen laid down about a hundred yards from the beach hid the invaders and their fleet. It also hid the work that had been going on since well before dawn. Companies of men were now working hurriedly to finish the job, for the Brotherhood of Diablo and their auxiliary forces had come up sooner than expected. It was still morning.

The pits were very deep; anything falling into them would build up considerable momentum before hitting bottom. In fact, what they would hit were embedded razor-sharp steel beams. Not even a Mog could survive such a fall. The last reed mats hiding the pits were even now being covered with sand.

Gunnar led the first skirmish, on a hillside about two hundred yards from the beach. The shock troops of the Brotherhood of Diablo were merely a wretched horde of ill-armed slaves, driven forward onto the pikes of the enemy by the threat of instant death from behind. Their slaughter was pathetic; nonetheless they took a toll of their own, even driving gaps here and there through the thin line of defenders. Then the Rathugs themselves charged, behind a screen of Mogs.

But Gunnar had a screen of his own, the smoke

screen. He signaled to his hornmen the instant the line of Mogs and Rathugs began to move forward. His slingers and pikemen retreated through the smoke—and kept on running. Guides led them through the field of concealed pits, and they immediately began to launch the beached galleys and transports as fast as possible. It looked like they were fleeing in panic.

Gunnar himself was the last to retreat through the smoke screen; his heavy trot left him far behind. There were still a few men working to erase the footprints between the concealed pits, but only a single guide stood waiting to lead him down a safe path. Rollo took him by the hand.

"You're not very swift, are you, Pa?" he said.

"I'll show you how swift I am, if I hear one more crack like that."

At that moment the line of Mogs and Rathugs charged through the wall of smoke like a legion of hideous demons emerging from the underworld. They hesitated in suspicion. Then their leaders saw the beach filled with thousands of men launching their ships in panic to flee. A tremendous shout thundered through the clouds of smoke; fifty elephantine Mogs and a thousand Rathugs charged out onto the beach.

Most of the ships had already been launched; only those directly behind the concealed pits were still being shoved into the water. But not even the Rathug captains noticed that the transports out at sea had divided in a pincers movement.

Gunnar still preferred his mighty warclub, but his first look at a Mog told him that it was not something he would want to fight up close. Crates of pikes and throwing-hatchets lay ready at hand, and he joined the line of skirmishers. The barrage slowed the charge of the Rathugs; they dropped back to let the Mogs take the brunt.

What they took instead were bladed steel beams as, one after another, they plunged into the concealed pits.

Meanwhile, screened by headlands far down the beach in both directions, thousands of armed men began to disembark and sweep inland behind the army of Rathugs. The battlefield had been chosen with great care.

"Pa, look!" cried Rollo.

"I thought I sent you aboard with—"

"No, look! One of the Mogs got through!"

Gunnar turned and saw that one of the monstrous humanoids had charged into the surf and seized one of the galleys before it was fully launched. Raging, tearing great chunks from the hull, it was dragging the helpless ship back onto the shore. Gunnar snatched up an armload of hatchets and shambled down the beach at his fastest trot.

The host of Rathugs had been balked by the pits, and before they could regroup they found themselves completely surrounded. Driven into a compact mass, only those in the outermost circle were able to fight back; those at the center could not even defend themselves from the terrible rain of pikes, slingstones, and throwing-hatchets. Although their army was outnumbered only two to one, the Rathugs in the outermost circle were assailed by at least ten times those odds.

As he approached, Gunnar saw that the Mog already had several knives and hatchets embedded in its flesh. Screaming in rage, it was tearing the doomed ship to pieces; torn limbs lay in bloody gobbets on the sand, for any of the crew that tried to leap over the side was instantly pounced on by the Mog and dismembered like an insect.

Gunnar flung a hatchet straight into the monster's back, then another. As it whirled around, pain and fury contorting its hideous features, Gunnar flung a hatchet point blank into its face. Then he was smashed against the side of the ship, momentarily stunned. But the Mog had been blinded; screaming and clawing at its face, it tried to tear the hatchet away.

Then Gunnar was on his feet again. He would have preferred his mighty warclub, but he swung his last remaining hatchet with all his might, putting the full weight of his back and shoulders and both arms into every blow.

Again and again the sharp blade gouged deeply into the flesh of the blinded, raging giant. Again he was smashed to the ground. Again he was on his feet and swinging with all his might. But the Mog's thick skull plates were like a steel helmet—until at last a blow caught it directly between the eyes.

Then all at once Gunnar was alone—dazed, bloody,

staggering drunkenly into the surf. He had a vague idea of shoving the damaged galley off the beach, but for several moments he could not find it anywhere. Then people were all around him, cheering, rejoicing, shouting his praises. . . .

It was mid-afternoon when he awoke. A single lamp burned in the ship's cabin. He was sure that he had never actually lost consciousness; but neither could he remember exactly how he got there. Someone had removed his leather shirt, and a girl was gently sponging his big hairy chest. Then he realized that the water in her basin was red.

"Have I been wounded?" he cried, sitting up.

The girl was so startled that she almost knocked over the basin. "No, you were covered with the giant's blood. You killed him all by yourself."

He noticed that her eyes were wide with admiration. He also noticed that she was about eighteen, with a pretty face and long slender legs. Then he recognized her as one of his own signal-girls.

"Thank you for your attention, Shana. Have you a towel I can dry myself . . . thank you, dear." He leered at her, and she blushed, obviously quite pleased that he had remembered her name. "Is that cabin door locked?"

"Yes, I told the captain you shouldn't be disturbed. That you killed the giant all by yourself and needed rest. Did I do right?"

"You did just right, dear," he said, affectionately patting her bottom.

"How's your hand now?" asked Eva.

Jana touched the bandage gingerly and wriggled her fingers. "I think it will be all right again in a couple of days. I just scaped it on a rock when I fell down. It's not really a battle wound."

"It could have been if that Rathug had caught you."

Jana nodded ruefully. "Or if you and those pikemen hadn't come running up when you did. But I won't wander off like that anymore. I've learned my lesson."

"I doubt it," said Eva.

It was evening; the gibbous moon was already visible in the darkening sky; torches and bonfires blazed the entire length of the beach. The pits that had been the deathtraps of the Mogs now served as the graves of the Brotherhood of Diablo; those thrown in and covered over with sand had not been checked too carefully for signs of life. None had survived.

"That was a very clever plan," said Jana, as they walked down the beach toward the flagship. "Driving them all together like that, so the ones at the center couldn't even fight. And I know it wasn't Margo's idea, this time."

"No," said Eva, "it was Hannibal's, thousands of years ago. He used it to destroy an entire Roman army. Is Willie still so far away?"

"Maybe even farther. I think he must be somewhere on the other side of the Rath of Diablo now. He started moving away about two hours ago. You'd think they'd start coming this way the minute they knew we won the battle."

"Assuming they knew that we did indeed win the battle. It was over before noon, and if they started moving away only a couple of hours ago—"

"Just about how long it would take scouts to reach them," cried Jana. "But they must have seen. . . . Oh, no!"

"What's wrong?"

"The smoke screen! They probably couldn't see anything."

"Or maybe the wrong things. Where's Stinky?"

After a minute: "On the flagship where we're going. But he can't take a message alone, if that's what you're thinking."

"No, he'll need help. Somebody who knows the island, somebody who could at least . . . Where's Korso?"

"Same place. I'd go myself, if Buck was still here."

"Let me go!" cried a voice behind them. "I'm faster than anybody except Stinky, and of course Derek himself."

"You'd better check with your father, Rollo," said Eva. "This will be a very dangerous mission."

"I'll check right now," he cried, and disappeared into the night.

The flagship had been dragged onto the beach; its

deck was brightly lighted with torches. Margo sat on a dais, surrounded by a throng of her worshiping admirers, like a living idol; her silken robes and painted face made her seem truly formidable. She rendered her decisions with sibyl-like assurance, and each petitioner in turn bowed almost to the deck and backed obsequiously from her presence.

"I think the other ceremonies are much nicer," said Jana, nodding toward the crowd out on the beach itself.

The people rescued from the Children of Satan had already begun to carry their ministry through the lands, even those dominated by the Brotherhood of Diablo. A tabernacle had been erected just down the beach, and the candles on its altar glimmered through the darkness. Hundreds of men and women had gathered around, and their psalms of thanksgiving praised God for granting them victory over the Brotherhood of Diablo.

"It's very beautiful," Eva said thoughtfully. "And very profound. But this was only one small victory in a great war."

"Oh, I wanted to talk to you about that. I heard that Margo just wants to blockade the island, now that we control the seas. She said something about time fighting our battles for us, because Diablo only produces a small part of the food it consumes."

"Yes, that was her advice."

"But, Eva, there are thousands and thousands of

slaves in the Rath of Diablo, and you know what would happen to them.''

''That's why I sent the fleet off this afternoon. Colinga Harbor is now deserted, and we may be able to salvage some of the cannons there. We have some walls to knock down.''

''I'd like to do some knocking down of my own—if I was only a little bigger. Look at her up there! I think she's got her own ideas about whose praises should be sung.''

''It's all right,'' cried Rollo, skidding to a halt on the sand. ''My father didn't say a single word against my going.''

Which was true. Although Gunnar might have had a few words to say if he had ever been asked. But he was still being attended to by one of the signal-girls, and Rollo had decided that it would not be prudent to disturb him just now merely to ask a question. Besides, he might have said no.

Chapter 11: No Communication

"You sure you know what you're d-doing, Korso?" whispered Stinky.

They had been traveling since well before dawn over the weird terrain of Diablo; in many places it was like a semi-tropical lowland jungle that had just sprouted mysteriously on a mountain top. It was now late afternoon; billowy white clouds tumbled through the sky—evidently there were strong winds overhead—and the terrain was now almost impassably rugged.

Korso whispered impatiently, "I told you already that I was in a labor camp near here. This is the only way past the Rath of Diablo for fifty miles around."

"Fifty miles ain't so far. That b-bridge looks mighty shaky to me, and who knows what's in that t-t-tunnel. Gunks, probably."

The trestlework of the old railroad bridge was badly decayed, but there was no other way apparent across the gorge. The sound of rushing water rose from far below. The rusted tracks led straight into a black tunnel.

"I wish that boy wasn't always running off like that," said Korso. "Anything that looks dangerous, and right away he wants to try it."

"Rollo's always b-been like that," said Stinky. "Do you think maybe w-we should have brought a lantern? Or c-c-candles? Looks mighty dark in that tunnel. Maybe the m-middle's collapsed."

"We'll just follow the tracks inside. We used it a couple of times when I was in the labor camp. It goes straight through to the other side of the mountain."

"Did you use that b-bridge too? Don't look like it would h-hold the weight of one of them b-big fat Rathugs. I just hope . . . There's Rollo! He's w-waving to us."

"Then let's go."

"Still d-don't like the looks of it," muttered Stinky.

They picked their way over the rotten trestles of the bridge and joined Rollo at the mouth of the tunnel. He had already cut three wooden canes for them.

"We can use these to feel our way like blind men," he whispered. "There's not a glimmer of light inside."

"What about Gunks?" said Stinky, peering doubtfully into the black tunnel. "Looks to m-me like the perfect place to b-b-be grabbed by Gunks and ate up. Nasty things!''

"Let's go," said Rollo. "Our message for Derek the Hunter must be very important. There are no Gunks here, Stinky. We left them all behind us at Saluston."

"So you s-say," muttered Stinky, following them into the tunnel. The daylight reached barely ten yards inside, and they were soon in pitch blackness. "But it sure l-looks like Gunk country to m-m-me."

"Don't be afraid," said Rollo, leading the way.

"Ain't afraid of n-nothing, so long as I got r-running room. How long is this thing anyway, Korso?"

"A little over a mile. These are the mountains surrounding the Rath of Diablo. This tunnel will carry us to the other side."

By running their canes along the tracks they moved straight on without having to grope. Wood hissing on rusty metal, and the crunch of their boots, were the only sounds. But it still took them nearly an hour to work their way through the tunnel. The gray mouth of the exit was actually in sight when they were jumped from behind.

There was no chance to fight back. Before they knew what was happening they found themselves bound with stout ropes and blindfolded. Whoever was dragging them down the tunnel was not very gentle about it.

"Told you so!" Stinky wailed plaintively. "Now w-we're going to get ate up by Gunks!"

Then a rough hand was clapped over his mouth.

"What a wonderful idea!" Willie clapped his hands delightedly.

Derek smiled at his enthusiasm. "It's from a book called *Salammbo*, a story about slaves trying to capture the stronghold of their former masters."

"Just like us!" he cried. "But I still wish we could somehow get close enough so I could talk to Jana again. What about that place on the north coast where we talked the last time?"

It was still late afternoon. The clatter of chisels, crowbars, and sledge-hammers resounded through the depths of the ravine. It was over fifty yards across and the arches of the old aqueduct were silhouetted against the billowy white clouds tumbling through the sky overhead. A squad of men worked furiously at its destruction.

"Jana's still near the place where the invasion was beaten back, isn't she?" Derek asked.

Willie nodded. "But I can just barely find her. I wish those scouts could have stayed a little longer."

"They didn't dare. Once the Rathug army drove our forces from the beach—and let's hope that most of them embarked in time—they would surely have started combing the hills for fugitives. The scouts might have been caught and tortured."

"They said that they could see at least some of our

ships pulling away from shore, even though there was a lot of smoke. Maybe the whole fleet got away,'' he added hopefully.

''And maybe they're still there, waiting for a chance to land again. Why else would Jana still be there?'' He glanced up at his squad of workmen. ''Somehow we have to draw the Rathug army back from the coast—and soon. Nothing is so likely to shake them as a lack of water. We can't cut off their food supply,'' he added with disgust.

''And this idea about the aqueduct comes from a book? Jana said that you read lots of books. The Rathugs always ripped them up and burned them. All they ever think about is drilling with weapons or horrible banquets or their fat women. And Soswa.''

''Soswa?''

''I've never actually seen one of the Rathagon's horror shows, but I've overheard some captains talking about them. I think these shows are only for the highest leaders of the Brotherhood of Diablo. All kinds of horror and nastiness, and this Soswa is supposed to be the biggest horror of all. Somehow he's supposed to be able to control people's minds. Ugh!'' He shuddered. ''Let's talk about something else. For instance, how long do you think it will take those messengers you sent to reach Jana and the others?''

''At least three or four days. All roads to the coast must be blocked by now, so they have to circle far to the north. How they're going to contact our ships, I don't know." He sighed. "And there's no way you can find Eva at this distance?"

He shook his head. "I can't even find the army of Rathugs anymore. But I'm sure she's all right. Remember how worried you were the last time, and then Jana told me that Eva had merely sailed north to organize the Fisherfolk."

"Well, she can't organize anything now, until we draw the Rathug army back from the coast. And that means creating as much havoc inside the Rath of Diablo as we can." He shrugged. "I don't know what else we can do."

"I wish I knew more about it. But they kept me in a cage, and whenever I got loose they would always catch me right away—then stick me with needles and keep me from falling asleep. I don't even know where these cisterns are, that you were talking about."

"I've already got a pretty good picture of this place, from escaped slaves. In fact, two of them are coming with us as guides. I just need you to warn me if we get too close to a Mog or Rathug."

"Don't worry about that," said Willie.

A man approached and bowed deferentially. "We are ready, Derek."

This was a development that Derek had not foreseen. Although he had tried to eliminate all unnecessary hierarchy, his followers had turned his name into a kind of title. They addressed him "Derek" as men had once used the titles "Lord" or "King."

"Tell the captain to proceed."

The aqueduct was hurriedly cleared of men. It had been cut and broken through to the point of collapse in several places; stout cables were fastened to all the critical supports.

"Let's go, Buck!" said Derek, and they moved a safe distance up the ravine.

"I still can't figure out how he can see with his eyes closed all day," said Willie. "Aren't we going back to the camp at all, then?"

Derek had reassembled his entire guerilla army, now several hundred strong, the moment the Brotherhood of Diablo had drawn off their own forces to repel the invasion. But it would be suicidal for so few men even to make a show of attacking the great, sprawling fortress of the Rathagon; their destruction might even release more Mogs and Rathugs to join the army defending the coast. He might use them to harry supplies and reinforcements, however; and he had taken precautions to block the movement of spies and messengers. The rest he would have to do himself.

"The guides we're taking with us can also act as messengers," said Derek. "Although I don't see yet how we could use the rest of our own men against the Rath of Diablo."

Willie nodded. "They'd only be killed. But you never know, if maybe we do enough damage inside the Rath—"

At that moment there was a grinding rumble, and the aqueduct crashed down into the ravine; a silvery stream of water came rushing down the slopes. The men scrambled for safety. Willie grinned.

"The Rathagon will be thirsty pretty soon. But not soon enough," said Derek. "The cisterns inside the Rath are still full of enough water to last them for weeks." He beckoned to the two guides.

He made arrangements to harrass any repair party sent out, although it would probably be several days before it was discovered exactly where the aqueduct had been torn down. He also reaffirmed his orders to stop all possible spies or messengers. If he had no communications of his own, then neither would the Brotherhood of Diablo.

It was dusk when they at last emerged before the walls of the fortress. At the very heart of the Rath of Diablo loomed the guard-towers of the old prison. But over the years a swarm of crude structures—barbarously designed and constructed—had spread outward from the original citadel like a cancerous growth. The entire hideous sprawl was now some five or six miles around, encircled by crumbling walls and towers that had been unneeded to defend the invincible Brotherhood of Diablo for generations. But for some reason, the walls were now heavily guarded.

"There is only one way to approach unseen, Derek." The guide bowed respectfully as he used the title. "Through the midden that we told you about."

"We know the inside of the Rath very well, Derek." The second guide also bowed. "Both of us were good workers, so were not butchered. We have worked in all parts of the Rath.''

Derek understood how much mere survival had cost these two men—both were emaciated and horribly scarred from the lash, one had had an eye torn from his face—and how much courage it had taken for them to return here with him.

He asked, ''What is this midden like?''

''You cannot see it from here, Derek. Just beyond that collapsed tower—see it there?—is an old ravine. All the filth and garbage of the Rath have been dumped there for many years. None go there, for it is a foul and terrible place. The guards avoid it because of the stench.'' He shrugged apologetically. ''It is the only way of approaching the walls unseen. At least, in daylight. But if we wait until just before morning—''

''There's no time,'' said Derek. ''Lead the way.''

''Whew, what a stink!'' cried Willie, holding his nose.

Then he buried his face in Buck's shaggy coat. Buck himself did not seem upset; some of his senses were keener than Willie's, and he had known about the smell the very moment that they emerged from the surrounding mountains. Derek gripped his hatchet as they approached.

''Are the main barracks or dog kennels on this side of the Rath?'' he asked one of the guides.

''No, Derek,'' he replied. ''Behind that wall are the larders and main kitchen. Over there is the butchery. The aqueduct enters the cisterns just beyond the collapsed tower.''

The cisterns must have stood well outside the bounds of the old prison. The new walls jogged outward to accommodate them, but there was no way of approaching that section unseen. Had anybody discovered yet that there was no more water flowing into the cisterns? If not, they would very soon.

The ravine had nearly been filled in; the level of the midden stood just below that of the valley around it, although some of the decaying mounds of refuse actually reached above. They did not have to worry about making too much noise. The midden was alive with gnawing, squealing, snarling creatures.

''You'd better get down, Willie,'' said Derek. ''We don't know what's running around here, and Buck may have to move fast.''

The mounds screened them from the walls above, but every step seemed to drive some slimy or scaly creature scuttling for cover. The squealing and snarling grew louder and more fierce. Suddenly a dark shape leapt straight at Willie's throat. But a lightning swipe of Buck's paw knocked it sprawling.

The huge rat-thing weighed a good thirty pounds. It was up instantly, rising on its hind legs, its filth-encrusted hair standing on end, its beady eyes red with malice. It hissed and snarled, baring its greenish fangs.

Buck feinted, and the rat-thing committed itself too soon. Almost faster than the eye could follow, he grabbed it by the back of its neck and shook it. They could hear the snap of its backbone.

As they hurried on, a vicious squabbling broke out behind them over the carcass. Huge rat-things, almost invisible in the gathering twilight, came scambling from all over the midden.

The two guides got them safely to the other side—although not even they suspected how lucky they had been. Perhaps daylight and the presence of Buck had been even more significant, for the Brotherhood of Diablo had not in fact overlooked this possible approach to their walls. It was well guarded—especially at night.

"There's a sentry about thirty yards that way, and three of them together. . . . Now one is moving off." Willie stood silently with his head bowed forward. They hugged the base of the wall not far from the collapsed tower; a guard would actually have to lean out from the wall and look straight down in order to see them. "The two that way are just standing there, about thirty or so yards away."

"The tower?"

After a moment: "Nobody there."

Still hugging the wall, they passed right under the two guards without being seen. But now they did have to worry about noise. The tower had been built of rough concrete blocks; its collapse had left a crude stairway to within a few feet of the opening above, but there was so much loose debris that Derek mistrusted the guides' ability to reach the top in silence. Nor could he leave them exposed here below.

First he led Buck and Willie to the top, without so much as a chipped pebble. Then he went back for the guides. They wouldn't like it, but it was the only safe way. One after another he carried them up the crude stairway in his arms. Then they were all sitting on a ledge, staring down into absolute darkness.

If the two guides were chagrined at being carried like babies by Derek the Hunter, they were even more chagrined when they were unable to tell him exactly what lay below.

Buck took it upon himself to investigate. Leaping into the blackness, he just seemed to vanish; there was no sound of his landing. Then two green lights suddenly appeared in the darkness less than eight feet below.

Derek sprang from the ledge with Willie in his arms. The two guides followed more cautiously, hanging by their hands from the ledge until they had worked up enough courage to let go. Buck's eyes were the only lights in the blackness all around them. Derek let him lead the way until they came upon a dim corridor.

There was a smell of fresh blood. From somewhere just ahead came the sound of a child sobbing.

Derek hesitated. He had long since learned that being a leader of men was no easy thing. The sound of a child sobbing amidst the reek of fresh blood was not something that he himself could ignore. But he knew that all his decisions now had to be made solely with regard to the invasion fleet, and the safety of the hundreds of men and women that he had left encamped near the old highway. It was very hard for him to turn away.

The guides knew exactly where they were now, and whispered the best route to the cisterns. Then Willie checked to make sure it was clear.

"That's funny," he said. "I didn't realize that so many Mogs and Rathugs had been sent to the coast. Although there are so many thousands of slaves here that it's hard to be sure. Except about the Mogs, of course. And Soswa. I always know where he is."

Derek looked thoughtfully down at him for a few moments, but then just shook his head. One job at a time. He nodded, and the guides silently led the way.

He found the great cisterns just as they had been described to him. There were sluice-gates to allow the cisterns to be cleaned, but the filthy, slime-encrusted stones indicated that they had not been properly cleaned for generations. A drainage tunnel carried off any overflow into subterranean depths, although the water level was already a few inches below maximum. The ripples on its oily surface seemed to be made by living creatures.

The domed ceiling was so low that even Willie had to bow his head as he walked. Lanterns glowed dully along one wall. At first Derek could not find any machinery for opening the sluice-gates. He assumed that it would be something like the windlass that raised the bridge at Saluston. No matter how rusty it was, he would surely be able to force open the gates a few inches. Even that would drain the cisterns, gradually.

But how gradually? The lanterns indicated that the cisterns were inspected regularly. He might have to stand guard for hours.

Then he discovered a corroded metal plate beside one of the sluice-gates. Using his hatchet as a lever, he pried it open. The spoked wheel inside was unrusted and surprisingly easy to turn. After only a few revolutions he heard the sound of tumbling water from somewhere far below.

He beckoned to one of the guides. "Here, you can handle this."

Soon he had every sluice-gate open—even Willie was able to turn one of the spoked wheels—and the water cascaded down the subterranean drainage system with an ever-increasing roar. In fact, the noise was now so loud that it would surely be investigated before much longer. They all turned their wheels as fast as they could.

Meanwhile Buck paced nervously up and back along the top of the wall. The water level was dropping fast, and he seemed confused about where it was going. But the cisterns were enormous, and it would still take some time for them to drain completely.

"Trouble!" cried Willie. He said something else,

but the thunderous rush of the waters was too loud. Derek ran over to him. "Two Rathugs coming from that way! And fast!"

Derek sent them all—including Buck—back into the dark passageway. If the guards understood what was happening, they could still save much of their water supply. He was determined to hold them in combat if necessary until the cisterns had emptied. There was too much noise for any cries of alarm to be heard very far.

At that moment two huge Rathugs charged into the domed enclosure, but for several precious minutes they just stared dumbfounded at the receding waters below. At last they drew their swords and charged as ferociously around the rim of the cisterns as the low ceiling allowed, shouting things that neither could hear in the roar of water. Then they just stared down into the emptying cisterns again; evidently there were no regulations governing such an event. Finally they hurried off in search of somebody to give them orders. There is always a price to pay for too much discipline. . . .

Derek got the others back to the collapsed tower as fast as he could. The enterprise had thus far been a complete success, but he realized now that it was still not enough. Given time the Brotherhood of Diablo would rebuild their fleet, their foundries and machines and cannons; nor would they ever again be caught by surprise. They must not be given that time. No matter what the price, their main army must somehow be lured back from the coast, so that Eva could land her invasion forces.

"If you're staying, so am I." Willie had guessed what he was thinking. "I know the inside of the Rath pretty well—some parts of it anyway."

"Do you know yet how many Rathugs are still here?"

He grinned. "Not enough to go out and chase our army, if that's what you're thinking."

Derek nodded: that was indeed what he had been thinking. Perhaps the Rathagon had dispatched the bulk of his forces to the coast, withholding a minimal number for guarding the walls and slave pens. Perhaps a demonstration beneath his very walls might cause him to recall his army, or enough of it to allow Eva's invasion forces to at least establish a beachhead. He gave the two guides a message for his captains: Bring up the entire guerilla army at dawn.

The last rays of twilight were falling as he hoisted the two men up to the ledge above. No matter how much noise they now made in picking their way down the stairway of rubble, they would probably not be pursued. A pair of escaping slaves were not the Rathagon's main problem now, and it turned out that he really had few men to spare. Derek hoped soon to give him a lot more problems—and a lot more escaping slaves.

In fact the two men crept back into the midden completely unnoticed, at least by the guards on the wall. But it was evening now, and they no longer had Buck with them.

They drew their swords, but had to concentrate on finding their way in the dark. Neither was aware of the tiny red lights converging stealthily on them from all directions.

Then something warm and slimy stung one of them on the leg. He gasped in pain. Whirling around, he met a whole galaxy of tiny red lights flying at him from all sides at once. Then both men were overwhelmed by a hissing, snarling, squealing mass of soft bodies. The message died with them.

Chapter 12: The Butchery

"Feel that f-fire?" moaned Stinky. "You know what that's for, d-don't you? Supper t-time for Gunks—and we're the supper."

"I told you to shut up!" growled somebody above him, and he was cuffed on the head.

He lay trussed and blindfolded on the ground, between Rollo and Korso. They had all been cuffed or kicked into silence whenever they tried to protest; Stinky alone still had to be reminded from time to time. They were uncomfortably close to a blazing campfire.

Rollo determined that in the future—if indeed he had a future—he would always do his thinking before the event, not during or after. If the old railroad tunnel was the shortest means of outflanking the Rath of Diablo, then of course it would be guarded. Derek the Hunter had not survived so many months on Diablo, building a formidable guerilla army, by being careless. It was stupid to have thought that he would just let them stroll into his camp unannounced; they should have tried to contact his outposts first. Now these oafish guards would not even let them talk.

From snatches of conversation that he had overheard, he guessed that these men were escaped slaves who had only recently joined Derek's army. They were anxious to prove themselves, and were hence over-zealous in carrying out their orders. He also guessed, from their continued talk about spies, that the Brother-hood of Diablo had tried to infiltrate them before now.

But the most important thing he had overheard was that the guard would soon be changed. The surly lout now guarding them cursed and kicked anybody who dared open his mouth. There was no talking to him; perhaps the new guard would be more reasonable. They had already lost hours of precious time.

He had a plan for getting the new guard's attention, but it would probably fail unless he could keep the others quiet. Any more whining or protesting while they changed the guards, and they could expect only more curses and kicks for the rest of the night. Then what? He had heard somewhere that spies were al-ways executed at dawn. Somehow he had to warn Korso and Stinky not to say anything under any circumstances.

Then he heard the guard moving away and he quickly whispered, "Listen, you two. They'll be changing the guard soon, but you mustn't say anything. Not a word. It's very important—"

"Plotting while my back is turned!"

The guard ran over to them and kicked Rollo in the side, knocking the wind out of him. He gasped painfully, trying to get his breath back. There was nothing more that he could do now—until they changed the guard. He only hoped that the others had been quick enough to understand him.

The minutes dragged slowly by. He wished that they had not been dumped so close to the fire.

Then footsteps approached. "So these three spies didn't run off on you after all," said a strange voice.

"Don't worry about me," said the surly guard. "But keep your eye on that kid. Plotting little sneak!"

"Can't be twelve years old," the new guard said doubtfully. "None of 'em look like much to me."

"It's your neck if they get loose," said the surly guard, moving away. "Not mine."

Rollo held his breath. He could hear the footsteps of their former guard growing fainter and fainter. If only Korso and Stinky would keep their mouths shut for a couple of minutes longer. . . .

"So now you're a bandit, you snaggle-toothed bucket of guts," Korso said sarcastically.

Rollo's heart sank. There went their last chance. All that they could expect now were more kicks, more cuffs, more precious time lost. He despaired of ever getting their message through to Derek the Hunter.

But then he heard the guard chuckling.

"Well, well, if it ain't my old benchmate. We all thought your ship went down last year, when it never came back." He laughed softly. "I don't care how much blubber you've put on, Korso. I'd know that fish mouth of yours anywhere."

"Dom, you've got to untie us," said Korso. "We've got to reach Derek the Hunter as soon as possible. We have important messages for him."

"Well, we get relieved here the day after tomorrow. I don't know if we're returning to the main camp or not. But I know you're no spy, Korso, and I'll vouch for you."

"Dom, believe me, it's important. Very important. Have I ever lied to you?"

"Sure, plenty of times."

"I mean, about something really important."

"No, can't say you ever did that. But you got to understand our position, Korso. Since the invasion was thrown back, it's important that any spies or messengers—"

"It wasn't thrown back!" cried Korso. "You mean that Derek the Hunter believes that our invasion was defeated?"

"That's what the scouts told him. Heard 'em say so myself."

"Get your captain at once, Dom. Please don't

argue. We destroyed the whole army of the Brotherhood of Diablo, even the Mogs. Eva is preparing to march inland in just three days. We've got to tell Derek the Hunter before he withdraws his forces to the other side of the island."

"He hasn't done that yet, but I heard he's up to something desperate. Him and that little mascot and his dog-thing are going to try and get inside the Rath of Diablo by themselves. We thought you people were thrown back into the sea. Well, well, this is good news."

Korso groaned. "Inside the Rath of Diablo!"

"We've all been kind of worried about that, Korso. He said he was going to send messengers back. But if he did, none of us has heard about it."

"Eva can't wait three days to march!" Rollo cried suddenly. "She has to be told what's happened to Derek, and right away!"

"He's right, Dom," said Korso. "Get your captain, hurry!"

"But he's sleeping, Korso. If I wake him now he'll grouch and snarl like an old Rathug."

"Dom, can't you understand—"

"All right, all right. But if this is a trick, Korso, the captain will be the end of me. Probably both of us." He muttered as he shuffled out of earshot, "He used to be kind of a nice guy too—until they made him a captain."

"You m-mean they ain't Gunks?" said Stinky. "Then why did they jump us like that in the d-dark?

Never would have c-c-caught me if I'd had any running room.''

''Save your breath,'' said Rollo. ''You might be doing a lot of running very soon.''

''Can't r-run my best the way we come. Not with all them rocks and gorges and bridges that might fall down. Hard enough j-just to walk.''

Then several people were hurrying their way; one of them sounded very grouchy and ill-humored indeed.

''Rowed on the same bench with him, captain,'' Dom explained. ''He says the invasion was a success. Destroyed the whole Rathug army, even the Mogs.''

''The Mogs?'' growled the captain. ''Do you expect me to believe—''

''It's true,'' cried Korso. ''We dug pits with sharpened metal beams at the bottom.''

''Maybe Derek the Hunter has returned to the main camp by now, captain,'' Dom suggested, ''or sent messengers back, like he said he would.''

''Take off their blindfolds, but don't untie them yet.''

They found themselves looking up at a husky, dark-bearded man with arms that barely reached down to his waist. But he had a very sharp knife in his hand, and a very mean look in his eye.

''I use this knife for skinning rabbits, but I can use it for skinning other things too. Understand? All right, untie them. Dom, you're in charge until I get back.''

"We'll be shorthanded, captain. Want me to wake up the other watch?"

"Good idea. I'll probably be back by morning." He looked significantly at the three messengers. "Unless I have a job of skinning to do. Let's get moving!"

The child had stopped sobbing, but as Derek and Willie crept up the dim, smoky corridor the murmur of people moaning and whimpering grew louder. So did the clanking of metal. The reek of fresh blood thickened the air like an invisible fog. Buck's hackles rose and his shoulders hunched forward, as if preparing to spring.

Just ahead a lighted doorway opened into the corridor. Then a metal door grated open somewhere inside the doorway, and a man's weak voice pleaded pathetically; the sounds of a brief struggle were followed by the slow clanking of a chain-hoist. Suddenly the man's voice grew clotted, as if he were drowning in some thick fluid. There was a splattering sound in a tub or large bucket, and the chain-hoist began to clank rapidly.

Willie tugged at Derek's sleeve and whispered, "There are about twenty people next door. I think that one of them just died. But there's only one Rathug . . . just a minute!" He bowed his head slightly forward.

Then the metal door opened and shut again. "Take this next," boomed a deep voice.

"Yes, only a single Rathug," said Willie. "That sounds like him."

The chain-hoist clanked slowly as Derek crept up on the lighted doorway. This time he heard the voice of a young girl speaking with some strange accent. But she was not pleading; she was cursing her enemies. Then he heard her muttering a prayer.

"Pretty thing," said a weak, servile voice. "Surprised you didn't keep it for a little fun."

"It would rather bite and scratch," boomed the first voice. "That's why it's here. Now shut up and do your job, or you'll find yourself up there with the rest of 'em."

Derek peered cautiously around the corner—and froze. His breath caught in his throat; his mind reeled with loathing and disgust. Not even the horrors of the last days of Saluston had prepared him for so ghastly a scene.

It was a butcher's nightmare. Heavy wooden tables lined the walls of a large chamber; slave butchers in bloody aprons worked with sharp knives and cleavers, cutting meat. From the chain-hoist high above them men, women, and even children hung by their ankles, their life's blood draining from incisions in their throats into a trough below. This was the butchery of the Brotherhood of Diablo.

Not far from the door sat a bulbous Rathug with a shaven head and fleshy white jowls; he had his back turned, and toyed with the whip in his hands. There was a large wheeled cage nearby, like those used by the slave raiders; there were about a dozen people inside, moaning and whimpering pathetically.

Two slave butchers were dragging a young girl toward the chain-hoist; the Rathug pointed mockingly at it with his whip and laughed obscenely. The girl's face was swollen where somebody had punched her, and her naked body was covered with red wales. She had stopped struggling now, and made the sign of the cross as she prayed.

The butchers threw her roughly to the floor, already slick with blood, and started to fasten her ankles to a hook on the chain-hoist. It was a job that they never finished.

The chopping sound was thunderously loud, and the bulbous Rathug collapsed to the floor with his backbone severed. The butchers tying the girl to the hook never saw what cut them down, but the four slave butchers still cutting meat at the table did, and they threw down their tools and began to plead for mercy.

"Please! Please! We were only following orders!"

"Nobody who follows such orders is fit to live," said Derek, advancing on them with his bloody hatchet.

They tried to snatch up their knives and cleavers again, but it was a futile gesture. Derek killed three of them; the fourth dodged past him and ran out the door. There was no need to pursue him.

A muffled cry; then silence. A moment later Buck and Willie appeared in the doorway. The latter had been forced to witness many hideous spectacles by the Brotherhood of Diablo, but this was more appalling than he could bear. He buried his face in Buck's coat and wept.

Derek was just as appalled; the sight of a small child about Willie's size, hanging by her ankles with her throat cut, was almost unbearable. Was this the child that they had heard sobbing when they turned away to drain the cisterns? He tried to shake off the thought. The dead were beyond help; the living might still be saved.

He untied the girl's ankles and helped her to her feet. Bruised, beaten, smeared with blood, she had still not lost her courage. But those in the monstrous wheeled cage had evidently been ruled by the Brotherhood of Diablo much longer. There were seven women, four men and a boy still inside, too numb with fright to do anything but moan and whimper. Not all their scars were visible on their naked bodies.

At last Derek coaxed them out of the cage. He wanted to delay any kind of alarm being given as long as possible, and he set them to work clearing the bodies from sight. But he needed a lot more people than this to do any appreciable damage inside the Rath of Diablo.

He asked Willie: "How do we reach the underground slave pens from here?"

"Well, they're that way, on the other side of the Rath, not too far from the Rathagon's citadel. I know that much. . . ."

"I know what you look for," cried the girl. She

had already cleansed herself, and her dark eyes shone with the light of vengeance.

But then she became confused and looked down in embarrassment. Derek removed his leather shirt and handed it to her. It was much too big for her; but it covered her nakedness, and her eyes thanked him as she slipped it on.

"People coming!" cried Willie. "Lots of them. Maybe even some Rathugs."

"Yes, the next batch for these filthy butchers, which you have gladly killed." She looked curiously down at Willie, uncertain how he could also have known this. "That cage is empty. Soon they wheel in the full cage. We must escape while we can."

Derek turned to Willie. "How many people are coming this way?"

After a moment: "About sixty, I'd guess. But now I can only find two Rathugs with them. They're closer now."

The girl looked even more curiously at Willie. But Derek was already organizing those he had released from the cage. The bodies had been shoved out of sight, and he got the boy and the women out of sight as well. Willie led the girl toward the door, but she hesitated to approach Buck, who sat on the threshold with his enormous eyes half closed against the light. Willie got him out of the way.

Less than ten minutes later the slaughter-room was filled with the heavy, grinding sound of a metal door sliding open. A Rathug weighing over four hundred pounds appeared with a whip of some light-colored skin in his great paw. He glanced arrogantly at the slave butchers working at the tables; they had their backs turned to him, and one of them was much larger than the others. But the Rathug only noticed that the assigned guard was missing, and he grinned maliciously. Somebody was going to get in trouble for this. He turned and barked an order.

Several emaciated slaves hurried into the slaughter-room and threw themselves against the empty cage with a kind of desperate exertion. At first it was too heavy for their feeble bodies, no matter how they strained. Then the slash of a whip encouraged them, and at last the cage began to move, its metal wheels grinding against the stone floor.

"Move, you vermin!" barked the Rathug. "If you can't do better than this, I'll put you in the next cage myself." His whip bit into their scrawny backs, slash after slash.

The wheeled cage ground heavily out the doorway. A few minutes later an even heavier grinding was heard; another whip cracked, another deep voice arrogantly barked commands. Then into the smoky light a new cage, mercilessly crammed with human beings, was heaved and tugged by a new gang of slaves. A wizened little man sat on top, steering it. From his own comfortable vantage point, he seemed maliciously amused by the frantic efforts of the slave gang below, by the moaning and whimpering of those crammed into the cage beneath him. He had evidently held this job a long time.

The second Rathug had dwarfish legs and was a leprous white, but he looked every bit as formidable as the other, and more agile. Both were too busy with the placing of the wheeled cage to notice the large butcher stealthily leave his table and glide toward them. He did not carry the usual butcher-knife in his hand, but a hatchet.

The two Rathugs were now the entire length of the cage apart, cursing and barking orders and slashing with their whips. Derek knew that he would have to be very fast—and very lucky. The Rathug with the dwarfish legs was closest to him, and he leapt forward, swinging his hatchet with both hands. Not even trying to catch the severed trunk, he sprang like a predator at the second Rathug—but he was still not quick enough.

A lifetime of military drill had made combat a second instinct, and the Rathug drew his sword and assumed a defensive posture in one smooth motion. He stood ready to face any conceivable danger before his conscious brain even realized the exact nature of his enemy. He deftly parried Derek's first blow, sending him staggering backwards against the wheeled cage.

Slowly they circled each other. Even the arrogant Rathug sensed that this would not be an easy fight; perhaps he even suspected the identity of his opponent. The moaning and whimpering in the cage had ceased;

the pathetic creatures inside were less stirred by hopes of escape than utterly dumbfounded that anybody would stand up to an Invincible. They watched the struggle as dumbly as so many cattle.

But the girl had also been watching from the doorway, and her reaction was much more aggressive. She burst into the chamber and raced for the nearest butcher-table. Gathering up as many butcher-knives and cleavers as she could carry, she took up her position just outside the range of the circling fighters.

A cleaver bit into the Rathug's lower back, and he started in pain. It was not a deep wound, but it momentarily distracted him. Derek leapt at him, swinging his hatchet. But again the blow was parried skilfully, and he was knocked off balance. As the Rathug glided forward a butcher-knife caught him square in the back of his leg. Then another cleaver glanced off his shoulder.

He whirled and charged at the girl with a quickness that almost caught her off guard. Her knives and cleavers clattered to the floor as she leapt out of range, but the Rathug dared not pursue. His mastery of martial drill ranked high even among the Brotherhood of Diablo, and he whirled and thrust with deadly precision. The girl's attack had distracted him for less than two seconds—but that is a long time in combat with such an opponent. Derek slipped past the sword thrust with lightning quickness, sank his hatchet into the Rathug's chest, and leapt aside.

As the Rathug staggered backwards, trying to tear

the hatchet from his chest, his helmet was snatched off from behind and a meat-cleaver split his skull. Derek also snatched up a cleaver, but the Rathug was already dead when he reached him. He restrained the girl from continuing to attack with a butcher-knife.

Then he heard a shriek of terror above him. The wizened old scoundrel who steered the wheeled cages was being dragged down by the slaves below. Derek started forward but the girl grabbed his arm.

"No, that is Garbis," she cried. "A spy who gave many over to death by these butchers."

In any case, it was already too late to save the wretch, who had now been dragged down and hacked to pieces by the angry slaves. Nor was there any more point in worrying about an alarm being given. He tore open the door of the wheeled cage and began pulling out the men and women inside. There was no time for coaxing.

Then he ran to the sliding door through which the cages were brought. There was no way of bolting it. As he turned away he saw Willie jumping up and down in the other doorway trying to get his attention. He could not hear the shrill little voice through the noise and confusion—he didn't have to. He knew exactly what Willie was trying to warn him about.

Ladders were their first need, but he could only find two of the necessary height. The slaves who had pushed the cages were less stupefied by what was happening than those liberated from inside, and he chose leaders from among them. Then he asked Willie to check on their escape route, and got explicit directions to the slave pens from the girl.

"It's all clear, Derek," Willie shouted back through the noise.

The reaction was startling. The whole ghastly chamber suddenly fell silent, and Derek found everybody staring at him in awe. Derek the Hunter! They would follow him anywhere. It now became a very simple matter to get them organized, and he had them collect all the torches and lanterns that they could carry.

Sending Willie on ahead with Buck, he himself led the way back to the collapsed tower. There were over sixty men, women, and children, all carrying torches or lanterns. The flight of so many slaves at once was sure to draw a horde of Rathugs in this direction, even though they would certainly not pursue them—at least tonight. The slave pens were on the opposite side of the Rath of Diablo.

Scrambling up the two ladders or hoisted onto the ledge from below, the slaves poured down the crude stairway of concrete blocks and rubble outside. Derek watched the burst of shining lights fan outward from the base of the tower; he was happy to see that the leaders he had chosen were guiding the people in at least the general direction of his camp. They would be cared for there.

Then the walls all around him erupted with angry cries of alarm; trumpets blasted, and heavy boots clumped and scraped and clattered. He turned and leaped into the darkness below.

Chapter 13: The Marathon

Most of the several hundred men and women in the guerilla army were still suffering from the effects of starvation and the lash. But the assemblage of patchwork tents was orderly; guards were posted along every approach to the camp, and shiny weapons were stacked ready for battle. It was still an hour before dawn, but the commander's tent was brightly lighted, and an anxious crowd filled the entrance.

"We can only suppose that Derek and his little mascot have been killed or captured by now—"

"No! No!" The tent rang with angry voices.

The old captain patiently held up his hands for silence. "Obviously we all pray that this is not true. But we've received no word, so we must now act on our own. Is it agreed that these messages are reliable?"

"Every w-word is the truth!" Stinky cried indignantly. "I'll t-take an oath on it."

"Take a bath instead," somebody said behind him, and there was a burst of laughter.

The old captain continued, "Derek told us about you. He said you were probably the fastest creature ever to run on two legs."

"Every word of that's true t-too." He glanced disdainfully back at those who had laughed at him.

"But what about four legs?" asked the captain.

"If they d-don't catch me quick, they w-won't."

"The old highway runs straight to the coast," the captain said thoughtfully. "I'm going to send messengers by other routes—just in case you don't make it—but it may take them days to get there. Derek himself sent messengers that way, but that was when we believed your invasion had been thrown back. Everything is different now."

"We haven't got days, captain," said Rollo. "If Derek is inside the Rath of Diablo, that can only mean—"

"I know what it means, son. But supposing . . ." He raised his hands for silence. "Supposing something has happened to him. Now I know that he ordered us to stay here until he sent word. But what if he can't? Or what if something happened to the messengers? I say, join our two armies together and attack."

The shout of approval was unanimous. Then a

commotion erupted near the entrance, and new shouting rang through the tent.

"He lives! Derek lives!"

The slaves liberated from the butchery had now begun to straggle into camp. Naked and bewildered, they were hurriedly shoved forward among the captains. The most interesting part of their report was the fact that they had not been pursued. This was so unlike the usual cruel vindictiveness of the Brotherhood of Diablo that they were all encouraged.

"That settles it!" cried the old captain. "We march at once!"

Shouts, cheers, and the clatter of weapons resounded through the camp; the avenue outside the conference tent streamed with torches as captains hurried off to rally their units; the shiny weapons were unstacked and passed from hand to hand. The dream of their forefathers had at last come true. They were marching on the Rath of Diablo!

"Can you run at night?" the old captain asked Stinky as they left the tent.

"Any time, any p-place. But what's that you said about f-four legs?"

"The old highway runs past the Rath of Diablo straight down to the coast. But there are guard-posts along the route—at least two that we know of—and they have dog-things."

"How f-far is it to the coast from h-h-here?"

"About thirty miles."

Stinky relaxed. "That ain't n-nothing. And the

doggies are p-probably tied up, so I'll be past 'em b-before they can even untie the ropes. Leastways, I hope so. Now how do I f-find this coast road?"

"Look down," said the old captain. "You're standing on it. Have you got your message straight?" Stinky repeated it for him. "Good. Have you had your breakfast yet?"

"I'll h-have it when I reach the coast, which w-won't take me no time at all." He nodded his round little head with determination. "I g-got a special reason for wanting to b-be a hero, you see."

They shouted encouragement as he trotted through the crowd; then stared in silent amazement as he vanished into the moonlight in a blur of arms and legs.

But the old highway was too treacherous in places for Stinky to run at his best speed. Cracks, debris slides, erosion, earthquake fissures broke the surface; he had to keep a wary eye on the road before him. He was past the first guard-post before he even heard the baying of dog-things. There was no pursuit. The Rathugs on guard probably never knew what had made their animals so restless.

Stinky's long, loping strides ate up the miles at an incredible rate, although he still had to be wary about his footing. Slowly the road before him grew easier to see, the treacherous places easier to avoid. It was morning, which meant that he too would soon be easier to see. But it was mostly downhill, and he was doing what he did best—running.

Then he reached a stretch cut through a series of rock spurs, and he had to be especially wary of loose debris on the pavement. He did not see the guard-post until he came running around the bend—and almost ran smack into it. There were angry shouts, and five huge Rathugs charged out of the brick building beside the road. Stinky put on a burst of speed and shot past them before they could block his way. A few missiles clattered harmlessly behind him.

He guffawed and turned his head to shout some insults, but what he saw was not at all funny. The Rathugs had already loosed their dog-things, and the lead he had on them was uncomfortably short; he threw back his round little head and ran for his life. Baying savagely, the whole pack came charging after him down the road.

He could now view the New Sea in the distance, many miles away and thousands of feet below him. Its waters were so clear and still that it looked like a turquoise mist hovering over a submerged network of roads, concrete channels, and railroad tracks; here and there he could even see drowned cities beneath the surface. Then he noticed the tiny ships, like a fleet of inverted nut-shells, seeming to hang in the air along the coast below.

He wished there wasn't so much debris on the road; one misstep and the dog-things would be on top of him in a snarling heap. They were already gaining on him.

He had raced against Buck while out hunting. He

needed about a ten-yard start for every hundred yards they ran; but after about a half mile at that pace he would usually begin to pull away. He doubted that the dog-things chasing him were as fast as Buck; but they were leaner and rangier, and thus might have greater endurance. It would be close. A lot depended on the condition of the road.

The pack had ceased baying, but he knew that they were still gaining on him. He could hear the click of their nails against the old concrete roadway. Were they tiring? Then he heard a yelp of pain hardly fifty yards behind him. The road was also treacherous for dog-things. The pack was now diminished by one.

There were sheer rock walls on either side of him, then open scrub, then the crumbling houses of some abandoned town. The dog-things were so close behind him now that he could hear their exhausted gasps for breath. He knew that they could not keep up the pace much longer. His wary eyes did not miss so much as a pebble on the road before him. A single false step could still lose the race for him.

It all ended quickly. The moment the dog-things ceased to gain on their quarry, they lost heart. At their own pace, they were capable of running for hours; but Stinky had forced them into so exhausting a chase that they had burned themselves out. He stopped and looked back.

Rusty signs flanked a crossroads; there was a deserted structure of cinder-block at one corner, and a jumble of abandoned vehicles at another. The sharp angle of the morning sunlight made everything unnaturally bright and vivid. Six big rangy dog-things sat in the middle of the road, their jaws hanging open, their slavering tongues lolling out with exhaustion as they panted desperately for breath.

"Haw! Haw!" Stinky laughed as he danced up and down with glee. "You ain't m-much, doggies! Now you know what r-real running is all about!" He threw back his round little head and guffawed.

Nor could he resist throwing a few stones at them as he danced tauntingly from one side of the road to the other; he even turned around and patted his bony rump in contempt. One of the dog-things managed a growl, but they were obviously finished. With a last guffaw, Stinky turned and trotted away.

But then he remembered the importance of his message, and once more opened his long, loping stride to his swiftest pace. It was all downhill now, and the road seemed to be in better condition. The ships of the fleet grew in size, but seemed more than ever to be magically suspended on a turquoise mist. The New Sea lay calm beneath a cloudless sky.

The encampment by the sea was an organized turmoil: loading and unloading, building wagons, distributing food and weapons, drilling. Stinky was astonished at the large number of cannons. Most looked like they had been in a fire or just fished out of the sea; Gunnar shambled angrily back and forth, encouraging the large crew he had working on them

But Stinky was given no time to watch. Somebody

must have seen him coming, because the moment he appeared on the beach he found Eva and little Jana expecting him. He took a deep breath, and delivered his message.

They both looked surprised; Eva frowned and for an instant closed her eyes in despair. But only for an instant. The next thing Stinky knew he was being hurried across the sand to the beached flagship; then the captains were around him, and he was telling them everything he knew. More frowns. More looks of despair.

''Like I s-said,'' he added. ''Everybody up there thought we g-g-got beat by the Rathugs. So Derek t-tried something desperate.''

While Eva and Margo discussed this new development with the captains, Jana drew Stinky aside.

''Did you actually see this Rath of Diablo?''

''Ran r-right past it in the moonlight.''

''What does it look like?''

''Big and ugly and m-miles around. Saw some Rathugs strutting on the w-walls just like their whole army didn't just get b-beat. No p-plan, far as I could see. It just kind of spreads out l-like a disease.''

''Does it look like a place where it would be easy to hide?''

''Hide? Bet you c-could hide an army inside. Looks like it's got m-more dark tunnels and such than Saluston ever had on its b-best day. Probably some Gunks sneaking around in the dark too. Wouldn't surprise m-me none.''

"I'm glad there are so many hiding places," Jana muttered to herself. Then she smiled and congratulated him. "You're a hero now, Lester. Marie will be very proud of you."

He raised his round little head and gazed toward the horizon. "I'm g-glad I'm a hero. Not for myself, of c-course. But you know how Marie is always r-reading about heroes and such." There was a whimsical look in his eye. "Pretty little g-gal!"

It was still early morning, and Eva got the bulk of her forces marching within the hour. There were still not enough wagons for all the supplies and equipment that had to be transported, and the men had to carry heavy packs. But there were no complaints. Two decisive victories over the Brotherhood of Diablo had had a wonderful effect on morale.

Nor did any of the crews left behind with Gunnar dare to complain. The cannons were not ready to be transported yet, and the barrels of powder salvaged from Colinga Harbor could only be carried in special wagons. These were still being constructed. But Gunnar encouraged his crews with such a barrage of growls, cuffs and goading sarcasm that their work became frenetic. He would have every cannon beneath the walls of the Rath of Diablo before dawn tomorrow—or know the reason why.

Chapter 14: The Dungeons of Diablo

There had only been two green lights in the darkness below when Derek sprang from the ledge. But a third light suddenly appeared just as he hit the stone floor. Leaping to his feet, he tore his hatchet from his belt, and braced himself for combat. But all that met him was Willie's merry laughter.

"She's on our side, Derek. I told her that she'd better escape while she could. . . ."

The girl held a lantern in her hand. "I can help you, Derek the Hunter."

"But you've already given me directions—"

"It is better if I lead you. In the Rath of Diablo it is easy to lose your way."

"That's certainly true," said Willie. "But right now I think we'd all better lose ourselves—and quick."

"What is your name?" asked Derek.

"Tereza. My people live to the south, in the Mountains of Tehachapee. But these filthy beasts hunt us with dog-things, and there are also traitors among us. I was betrayed." Her dark eyes flashed angrily. "I must have my chance for revenge."

Derek was slow to trust the abject slaves of Diablo, for all too many were ready to betray anybody, just to prolong their own misery. Only those who have known freedom can be trusted to fight for it. But whatever else the Brotherhood of Diablo had done to this poor girl, they had not broken her spirit.

He nodded. "All right, Tereza. Then let's get moving. You say that there's only one way in or out of these slave pens? That each is guarded by a Mog?"

They left the collapsed tower, and hurried silently down a deserted corridor that they had not used before. The girl seemed to know her way, and quickly grew accustomed to Buck.

"These Mogs are like nothing of this earth," she said. "But you are Derek the Hunter! Among my people far to the south your name is spoken with respect; among the slaves here in the Rath of Diablo it is a kind of prayer." She marched proudly beside him. "Yes, I will lead you, Derek the Hunter. Not even a Mog will long stand in your way."

Derek noticed the twinkle in Willie's eye. It was all very flattering, but he doubted that it would mean much to an actual Mog.

They cut across an open yard; weapons were locked

in racks along one whole wall. A drill field? But even more ominous was the sky. An almost imperceptible tinge of gray hovered just above the eastern walls; dawn was not far away. The girl also noticed this.

"The slaves will soon be taken from their pens," she whispered.

"All of them? What about the galley slaves? They were brought here after their fleet was burned."

"All now work repairing the walls and towers. We must hurry!"

"That's strange," Derek remarked, as they crossed the open yard. "Just a minute, Tereza." He turned to Willie. "Please check and see if you can find Jana."

He grinned. "Oh, I check on that all the time. She's still in the same place. Why?"

Derek shrugged. "I just don't understand why the Rathagon is now so concerned with his defenses. Didn't you say something about there being fewer Mogs than usual?"

"A lot fewer. The whole place feels empty. But there are so many thousands of slaves here . . ." He shrugged. "Our own army should be outside the walls in a little while."

"That's what I'm thinking. The Rathugs are probably worried about their empty cisterns already, and the crowd of escaping slaves—"

"And all the beasts you killed, Derek the Hunter." Then she gasped. "They will know you are here and try to hunt us down!"

"Not necessarily," said Derek. "They may only believe that the slaves somehow got out of their cage and overwhelmed the guards. I just wonder . . . Is there any movement of people in this direction, Willie?"

"You mean our army?" He was silent for a moment, then shook his head. "They don't seem to have moved at all. Didn't you want them to make some kind of demonstration after dawn?"

"They should be on the march by now." He glanced up at the graying sky. "I don't know what we can do until they get here. The Rathugs will now be getting their slaves ready for work, feeding them, and so forth."

"No, no," said the girl. "They never feed before work."

"That's right," said Willie. "They only feed them according to how much work they do, and how well the guards like them. And you know what happens to those who can't do enough work anymore."

"We'll just have to find some place to hide until our people get here," Derek decided at last. "The Rathugs may then have to return the slaves to their pens."

"So we can let them right out again?" cried Willie. Then he bowed his head slightly forward. "Oh, oh, Rathugs! That way! About ten of them, maybe eleven."

Derek quickly turned to the girl. "Do you know a

good hiding place near the slave pens? We may have to wait a while, perhaps hours.''

''Yes, I'll show you. This way.''

But Derek first turned to Willie, who shook his head. ''No, it can only be that way or, let me see, that way over there.''

''Can we reach the hiding place from those directions, Tereza?''

''From that way, yes.'' She looked curiously at Willie. ''But it will take longer.''

''That's not important now. All the other routes are blocked. Come on, Buck! Let's go!''

It was late morning when Willie suddenly opened his eyes. The loft stood at the very top of an abandoned tower, and sunlight shone through a hole in the roof. Nobody would be likely to search for them here; Tereza had certainly been right about that. In fact, the whole tower looked ready to collapse any minute now. He was still afraid of making any quick movements.

He had slept using Buck as a pillow. As he looked across the dim loft he saw that Derek was still asleep. Tereza sat by his side, gazing down at him with a strange look on her face. She had evidently decided to watch over him and keep the flies from bothering him while he slept. Then she noticed that Willie had his eyes open.

''Did the trumpets wake you?'' she whispered.

"Oh, we have awakened him!" There was now a distressed look in her eyes.

Derek sat up, yawned, and blinked sleepily. "What time is it?"

"Time to get up," said Willie. "We're being attacked." He laughed merrily at the alarmed look on Derek's face. "No, not here. The Rath of Diablo. Hear the trumpets?"

"Our army has come up!" Derek leapt to his feet and hurried to a boarded window. Standing on tiptoes, he peered down through a crack.

"Careful careful," cried Willie in alarm. "No, Buck, don't get up. . . ." He held his breath as the great beast rose and stretched. "This whole place is going to come tumbling down, if we're not careful."

"Looks like most of the defenders are now moving toward the northern wall," said Derek.

Willie added, "And the slaves are being herded back to . . . ow, my ears! What was that?"

"A cannon," said Derek. "But I'm pretty sure that most of their cannons were down at Colinga Harbor. Let's get moving."

"All right," said Willie. "But let's not move too fast. Are you sure those stairs will hold our weight again?"

"We'll go one at a time," said Derek, and they reached the bottom of the dark stairwell with nothing more than some dust and splinters falling on them.

The walls and towers of the old maximum-security

prison rose into the morning sunlight not far away. They were at the very heart of the Rath of Diablo.

Tereza glared angrily toward the citadel. "How I would like to put this knife into the heart of the Rathagon himself before I die!"

"That's where most of the Mogs are," added Willie. "And Soswa. And a lot of other weird creatures." He muttered, "I never have any trouble finding the citadel."

"Right now we just want to find the slave pens," said Derek. "We don't want the Rathagon to think that he can concentrate all his remaining forces on the northern wall. If we cause him enough trouble, he might even recall his army from the coast. Tereza?"

The last time that the girl left the area of the slave pens it had been in a cage. But she proved to be a bold and infallible guide: down crumbling stairways; through a labyrinth of dark corridors; even wading through a flooded tunnel deep underground, its slime-encrusted walls alive with crawling things. She was less intimidated by the water than Buck, who growled sullenly at getting his paws wet. Then they descended a long stone ramp. There was torchlight ahead. The air was dank and heavy with the musty reek of confinement.

"A Mog!" Willie cautioned them.

Derek immediately drew them aside. There were between two hundred and five hundred slaves in each of the pens; but a single Mog at the entrance made any other safeguard unnecessary. There could be no escape, either by force or even stealth, until the Mog was removed somehow.

But with a hatchet? It took a heavy pole-axe just to sever a Mog's backbone, and their skull-plates were too thick to rely on a blow from behind. When one ran amuck in battle the Rathug technique was to try and drive a heavy javelin or battle-axe directly between its eyes, the only sure target. But you only got one shot; even a Rathug would be torn to pieces if he missed. Derek could not think of a means of getting close enough even to attempt such a blow.

"I will help you, Derek the Hunter," whispered the girl. "I am not afraid."

Before he could stop her, she stripped off the leather shirt, tossed it to Willie, and stepped like a martyr out into the corridor. Her naked young body shone like burnished bronze in the torchlight as she strode fearlessly toward the slave pen. The Mog would spot her coming any moment now.

Derek could see immediately what the girl planned to do, and for once he did not enjoy his glorious reputation. She had committed him to an act more desperate than any he might have chosen himself. He pulled his head back so that he himself would not be spotted.

A menacing growl sounded somewhere down the corridor, and then the girl's voice could be heard speaking calmly. Derek kept his eyes on Willie, whose little head was bowed in concentration. At last he gave the signal: the girl had moved to the other side of the niche where the Mog had been standing. It would now have its back turned.

Derek gripped his hatchet and slipped out into the corridor. The Mog had also stepped out into the middle of the corridor, completely blocking it. Over nine feet tall and broad in proportion, its head came to within inches of the ceiling. It was looking down at something on the other side of it, growling ominously.

"A master brought me," the girl repeated. "I tell you again that he took me upstairs, then brought me down again. Ask him. There he is now."

The Mog turned stupidly around. Derek leapt straight at it, swinging his hatchet with both hands. The blade crashed into the beetling forehead just between the eyes.

Then Derek and the girl fled in opposite directions. The Mog's brain had been pierced; it was biologically dead. But until it actually fell it could still be terribly dangerous. Staggering drunkenly, it lurched toward Derek down the corridor. Suddenly it dropped like a felled tree.

Derek wrenched his hatchet loose and ran for the slave pen. Tereza was already there. Over three hundred abject wretches were herded together in a dank, airless dungeon; there was not even room enough for all to sit or lie down at the same time. A few had some rags of clothing, but most were naked. They had only just been returned from their work stations and were still settling down.

But Tereza had already informed those nearest the door what had happened, and the word quickly spread through the dungeon. A Mog killed! Derek the Hunter! Then Derek himself appeared in the doorway, and hundreds of upturned faces regarded him with silent awe. It reminded him of the first time that he returned to Saluston from the outside world with his quarry slung over his shoulders; a successful hunter. He handed his leather shirt back to the girl.

But she shook her head; not even her natural modesty could overcome her desire for vengeance. There were still four more slave pens nearby. Their entrances were so close together that they were guarded by only two Mogs. Derek was surprised at the small number of slaves.

"The rest are brought to the Rathagon," said Tereza, who had meanwhile been questioning those around her. "I have heard that there are several dungeons with barred doors beneath his citadel. Perhaps the galley slaves have been taken to one of these."

"The galley slaves!" cried Derek. Why would the Rathagon do that unless he was planning to escape? He shook his head. "I really don't understand what's going on. But we'd better see what we can do at the other slave pens while all the Rathagon's forces are occupied."

"Then come, Derek the Hunter," said the girl, with a strange light in her eyes. "I am not afraid." Once more she strode into the corridor like a martyr on the way to the stake.

Leaving the slaves to choose leaders from among themselves, he followed silently after her; he had to admit that he was probably more apprehensive about facing two more Mogs than she was. Willie hunched forward on Buck's back, deep in concentration.

The number of empty pens indicated how costly the Battle of the New Sea had been to the Rathagon—also how huge his army was at the coast. No wonder Eva had been compelled to re-embark her invasion force. But why had the Rathagon withdrawn his last galley slaves into the citadel?

Then he got a signal from Willie, and took a firm grip on his hatchet.

They killed the second Mog as deftly as the first; but the next had quicker reflexes. As Derek leapt straight at its forehead, it instinctively threw out one of its huge arms. He sunk the hatchet blade deep into the monster's brain, but was slammed against the concrete wall.

Too stunned to think clearly, Derek's instincts saved him. Instead of trying to crawl painfully away from the Mog, he rolled over and slipped between its legs. By the time it managed to turn around—half blinded and bouncing drunkenly from wall to wall—it could no longer reach him before it collapsed to the floor.

Dazed and shaken, he staggered to his feet. But the girl could not believe that he was badly injured—or ever could be.

"No," she said proudly, "you are Derek the Hunter."

She seemed to misinterpret the fixed gaze in his eyes, as she modestly covered her nakedness once more with his leather shirt. But her faith turned out to be justified—he was not badly injured. After a few minutes the cloudiness of his vision began to relent, and his mind to work clearly again.

But he had a greater problem than ever in getting the slaves to move. Beaten, tortured, emaciated, herded like the lowest of beast-things, most of them were too frightened and abject even to assist their own escape. Making free human beings out of wretches who had never known either freedom or humanity is an immense task, and Derek lost hours of precious time organizing them.

Meanwhile Willie concentrated solely on events in and around the Rath of Diablo. The guerilla army had moved somewhat further to the north—perhaps because of the cannons—but the Rathugs were still concentrated along the northern walls.

The few sentinels at the southern wall were easy to evade. Then thousands of men, women, and children were streaming from the Rath of Diablo into the afternoon sunlight.

Chapter 15: The Last Escape

The spies and Judases of the Brotherhood of Diablo were the best fed and treated of all the slaves. But the galley slaves had to be fed at least well enough to keep them fit for hard rowing. They were now being fed better than they ever had in their lives.

"For whatever reason they're being withdrawn to the citadel," Derek decided at last, "their liberation must in some way hurt the Rathagon. What else is down here?"

"The armories," said the girl. "All the armories of the Rathugs. And storerooms, many storerooms. This much I know from talking to people."

"What about the citadel itself, Willie?" asked Derek. "You've been inside it."

"Yes, but not this far underground. Most of the

time I was locked in a cage in the Rathagon's chambers, at the very top of the citadel. The horror shows I told you about take place somewhere down here. They never let me see even how they got down here themselves." He grinned. "Although I've got a pretty good idea how they did it. But haven't we done enough damage? Buck is getting hungry, and so am I."

"Perhaps you're right. Perhaps if we could somehow . . ." Then he nodded decisively. "Yes, we could use the galley slaves to damage these armories and storerooms, and then get out of here. Maybe we could even wreck their cannons on our way over the walls, although I don't think they have many left. But first we have to get into the citadel."

"I am sorry, Derek the Hunter." The girl hung her head. "I know not the way into the citadel from here."

"I don't think these galley slaves are actually inside the citadel," said Willie. "Very close, but not inside. Maybe there are just too many of them."

"There are no dungeons here outside the citadel," said the girl. "This much I know."

"But you said that there are large armories and storerooms near it," replied Derek. "Since the galley slaves were only brought here because of some emergency, perhaps one of these armories or storerooms—"

"The drill hall!" cried the girl. "It is where these filthy Rathugs drill when weather is bad, or at night.

I know the way, Derek the Hunter,'' she said, as if redeeming herself.

''Willie?'' Derek checked.

He was silent an unusually long time; at last he shook his head. ''Blocked in every direction. I don't know why there are now so many Rathugs running around down here, and not up on the northern walls. Maybe they're searching for us? With all the slaves escaping at once—''

They were startled by a wild clanging noise. The alarm! For an instant they believed that the Rathugs really had come down here to search for them—and had just succeeded.

''Check all around us, Willie,'' Derek whispered.

''I haven't done anything else for hours,'' he muttered. ''I certainly don't want to end up back in my cage.'' Then he was silent for several minutes, while they shrank deeper into their hiding place. ''That's funny,'' he exclaimed at last. ''Now they're all running for the upper levels. Something's up.''

''Have they opened any path to the galley slaves?''

After a moment: ''That way.''

Then the armories and weapon shops of the Brotherhood of Diablo were all around them. One corridor was blocked by a wall of rough concrete: the foundation of the old maximum-security prison. At last Willie signaled them to halt.

''See that entrance just ahead?'' he whispered. ''That's where they are.''

"Yes, yes," said Tereza, "the drill hall I tell you about. But I see no Mogs, or any guards at all."

"They must be inside with the galley slaves," said Willie. "I can't tell how many Rathugs there are in such a big crowd, but there are no Mogs at all. . . . No, there's still a few down here, but none very close."

"Wait here!" said Derek.

He leapt to his feet and darted silently the length of the corridor. At the entrance of the drill hall he dropped to his knees and peered warily around the corner; then he disappeared from sight. It was several minutes before he returned.

"They're chained in rows by their ankles, just as aboard ship. There are only two Rathugs, but any attack would cause a commotion."

"There are only a few Mogs down here," Willie reminded him.

"One would be enough. Let's get back to that last armory we passed. We'll need weapons, lots of weapons."

When they crept back toward the drill hall some time later, they had all the weapons that they could carry. Derek hoisted a full armload; the girl managed a surprising number of heavy pikes and javelins; even Willie struggled along behind with a pair of swords. But it was Buck who hauled the most formidable load of all, although he was obviously disgruntled about the sling rigged across his back.

Next came the mattresses. A small storeroom just

down the corridor from the drill-hall entrance had been improvised as sleeping quarters for the Rathug guards. Laying their weapons aside, Derek and the girl dragged two enormous, foul-smelling mattresses back toward the door. But their next move depended on the exact position of the Rathugs inside the drill hall itself. Leaving the others behind, Derek crept silently back down the corridor.

The vestibule of the drill hall was lined with weapon-racks, unfortunately empty. Derek crossed it and peered cautiously through the door.

One Rathug sat less than twenty feet away; but his face was in profile, and it would not be easy to take him unawares—nor possible to reach the ring of keys hanging on the wall behind him. The other Rathug, a squat, hirsute monstrosity with strange amphibian splayed feet, was inspecting the chains of the galley slaves at the far side of the big drill hall. There were over four hundred of them, and the animal stench was overpowering.

Then Derek heard a restive clatter out in the corridor and hurried to investigate. It was only Buck. Growing impatient with his heavy load of weapons, he was ignoring all Willie's efforts to keep him still. It took even Derek several minutes to quiet him down.

But as he turned away, Willie alerted him: "Wait, Derek. Somebody's coming."

They doused the lamp; but two big green lights still shone in the darkness. Derek quickly covered Buck's eyes with his hands—and waited. A few moments later a wheeled food-cart was pushed past the door by two slaves. Among various greasy stuffs lay a smoking joint of meat, evidently the guards' dinner. A dark Rathug strode arrogantly behind.

As the rattling of the cart died away, they could just perceive a heavy barrage of cannon fire; perhaps they felt the vibrations as much as heard them. It sounded like the Brotherhood of Diablo still had an imposing ordnance—far, far more imposing than Derek had suspected. Where could so many cannons have come from? In any case, silencing as many of them as possible now had to be their main objective.

Among so many hundreds of galley slaves there were surely some men of spirit who would help him sabotage the cannons. The abject could merely be sent fleeing over the southern wall, which would at least deprive the Rathagon of their services. The distant vibration of cannons grew more intense.

"Nothing close yet," Willie reported. "Don't worry, I'm checking around us all the time."

That there were now three Rathugs in the drill hall made their task far more difficult. But they dared not wait. How much longer would the alarm that had cleared the corridors last?

Derek lugged one of the heavy mattresses to the entrance and returned to help the girl with the other, keeping one eye on Willie for any sign of approaching danger. Then they quickly transported all the weapons into the vestibule, careful to keep Buck from making too much noise. Willie assured them in a whisper:

"Don't you worry about me or Buck—we'll do our jobs."

Derek nodded encouragingly, although he knew that everything really depended on the girl doing her job. He recrossed the vestibule and pushed and squeezed the two enormous mattresses until they completely blocked the entrance. It would now take a mighty commotion indeed to reach the ears of even a nearby Mog.

Hefting a thick javelin in each hand, Derek glanced back at the others. They nodded their readiness. Buck rolled his huge green eyes from one to the other, unsure yet about what was expected of him; but he caused no trouble.

Then Derek launched himself through the doorway. The Rathug sitting by the ring of keys now balanced a huge platter across his lap, gluttonously stuffing portions of food into his great slobbering maw with a clasp-knife. The javelin caught him square in the neck, and he fell choking and writhing to the floor. But the other two Rathugs were instantly on guard. Derek feinted with his second javelin, but did not throw it. He heard the jingle of keys behind him.

The Rathugs had only swords, and to charge a man with a javelin—a man who had just shown that he knew how to use it—could mean a serious wound for one of them, perhaps even death. They backed toward the wall where rows of shields and drill-weapons hung in racks.

Derek knew that he could not hold two armed Rathugs at bay for more than a couple of minutes—if that long. But the girl needed more time if she was to do her job. The whole drill hall now rang with shouts, cries, and the rattle of chains, but nothing would stop the two Rathugs once they were properly armed. Derek had to attempt a risky maneuver.

Feinting again and again with his last remaining javelin, he suddenly thrust it straight at the face of the nearest Rathug, causing him to throw up his sword in defense. Before he could recover, he found himself staggering backwards with a javelin in his chest; he bellowed with pain and anger. But instead of charging, the second Rathug only leapt for the weapon-rack.

This gave Derek his opportunity. The girl had already unlocked most of the chains, but these passed in series through rings on the slaves' ankles, and few men were actually free yet. Nor were they armed.

Buck was so excited that Willie was having trouble unloading the sling. And the weapons were heavy—at least, for Willie. Only five swords lay on the floor beside him.

"Cut the sling away!" cried Derek.

But he himself could not help, for the Rathug, now fully armed, came charging straight at him. He barely had time to snatch up another javelin.

He was on the defensive now. The Rathug's greater

size and strength, and a lifetime of martial drill, gave him overwhelming advantages. Derek could only dodge back and forth, feinting with his javelin, using his greater quickness to keep just out of range of the skilful, powerful thrusts.

But the Rathug was also aware that the galley slaves were being unchained; within minutes he might have hundreds of them rushing at him. Somehow he had to sound the alarm. He attempted a risky maneuver of his own, and Derek's javelin was knocked away.

Derek sprang out of range, but by the time he had recovered his balance, the Rathug was lumbering toward the door. Willie squeaked in fright and scurried out of reach. He had a sword in his hand; that was to cut away the sling on Buck's back, although all he had managed to do so far was to chase the excited beast around in circles. Then Buck did his own unloading.

An avalanche of weapons tumbled from the sling as he leapt at the fleeing Rathug, hitting him from behind just as he reached the door. He tried to shove the great beast away with his arm—and had it almost clawed off to the elbow. Then he tried to use his sword—and had half his face torn away.

"Buck, here!" Derek called him off.

His javelin caught the Rathug in the shoulder and drove him heavily against the wall. But most of the galley slaves were free by now, and at least some were not too dispirited to snatch up weapons and avenge themselves. The Rathug was hacked to pieces.

Derek hurried to block the doorway, afraid that a mob of shouting, howling slaves bursting through the corridors outside would attract the few Mogs still roaming underground. But the girl had meanwhile been quieting the excited men on her own, pointing to Derek and repeating his name like an incantation—Derek the Hunter, Derek the Hunter. Soon the entire hall fell into an awed silence.

Derek at last cut the strap holding Buck's sling and had Willie get him out of the way. The men were stronger and less abject than he had expected; evidently the pick of the last Rathug fleet, now unusually well fed. He distributed weapons and got them organized within minutes. The legend of Derek the Hunter seemed to affect them even more powerfully than their fear of the Brotherhood of Diablo.

First checking with Willie, he wrenched the mattresses from the entrance, then led a platoon of men back to the armories. The arms still there were neither of the first quality nor very plentiful. But he saw that every galley slave had at least some kind of weapon. The entire Rath of Diablo now seemed to tremble with distant explosions. Platoon by platoon, he sent the men upwards to do as much damage to the cannons as possible before escaping over the walls.

"Oh, Derek!" Willie came running toward him.

''Rathugs seem to be coming toward us from all directions. They must be deserting the walls.''

''But that doesn't make sense,'' cried Derek. ''Our forces are far too small. . . . Where are they now? You haven't checked on anything outside the Rath in a long time.''

Willie was silent for only a split second. ''Jana!'' he cried. ''Oh, Derek, she's here. Right outside the walls. And thousands more people are with her.''

''There's only one answer,'' Derek said at last. ''Our invasion forces have somehow gotten past the Rathug army at the coast, perhaps even defeated it. Is Jana close enough for you to talk?''

He shook his head. ''I already tried. Maybe it's because I'm so far underground and these walls. . . .'' He was silent for a moment. ''They're definitely coming this way! Rathugs!''

''Probably withdrawing to the citadel above us.'' He had just sent the last armed platoon toward the surface. Would it now be cut off? Would they themselves now be cut off? ''Is there any escape route still open?''

Willie pointed to their right, and Derek quickly set him on Buck's back. But now they were moving back toward the citadel, instead of away from it —and then even that route was blocked.

''A Mog!'' cried Willie.

''What's behind it?''

''Nothing as far as . . . oh, oh, it's coming straight this way!''

"And there's no other route still open? Then just hold onto Buck. Tereza, the moment you see an opening, take it. And keep moving, both of you."

Once more they passed a rough concrete section of the old prison's foundation; but this time Willie was frightened by something.

"Oh, Derek, Soswa is just on the other side of that wall. I've never been so close to him before. He's evil and terrible, and I have a feeling that somehow he knows we're out here."

"Somebody definitely knows we're out here," replied Derek, as they raced down the murky corridor. "They're searching for us now, blocking every exit."

Willie agreed. "Every way but this one is crowded with Mogs and Rathugs. There's only that single Mog in front of us."

"They probably didn't expect us to turn back toward the citadel. Keep going!"

"But, Derek, a Mog!"

"Just do what I told you."

There was no longer any chance of fighting their way out, nor even of hiding. But perhaps Willie and the girl might still be saved. . . .

"There it is!" cried Willie.

The monstrous form blocked the entire corridor; it lumbered straight at them, its great paws groping as if to tear them to pieces. Derek hurled his javelin into its hideous face, and leapt up at it swinging his hatchet with both hands.

But the Mog swept the javelin aside and crouched,

legs apart, to catch the puny creature hurtling toward it. Derek's hatchet ricocheted futilely off the Mog's thick skull-plates, and he was dashed against the wall.

But the monster was distracted just long enough for Buck to shoot between its outstretched legs, with Willie clinging to his back. As the Mog whirled around to grab him, a space opened along the wall, and the girl leapt through it and was gone.

But not Buck. He hesitated, his huge green eyes glowing fiercely in the darkness just down the corridor. He had seen his master knocked down, and not all Willie's tugging and pleading could get him to budge.

"Go, Buck!" Derek gasped. "Go, Buck! Go!"

Still uncertain, the great beast at last turned and raced up the corridor. Derek struggled to his feet, dazed and weaponless. He could hear a mob surging toward him from the other direction, but anything was better than facing a Mog. Perhaps he could still find something to defend himself with along the way.

But he only managed to stagger a few steps back up the corridor before he was snatched from behind like a helpless doll. The bone-crushing grip robbed him of breath; he felt his ribs cracking, and he tried to struggle. But the grip only grew tighter and tighter. Then there were hulking shapes all around him, and he lost consciousness.

Chapter 16: The Hidden Staircase

Doubling the size of an army quadruples its effectiveness. Eva could not remember exactly where she had read that particular formula, but it was a principle that she never forgot. Had the Brotherhood of Diablo joined all their scattered forces against her, the march inland might have taken days—perhaps even weeks—rather than just hours. One after the other, she threw the entire mass of her army against each Rathug outpost barring her path; one after the other, each was overwhelmed.

There are always fewer casualties when running toward the battlefield than away from it. This was another military formula that she never forgot, and not once did she allow herself to lose the initiative. She always attacked.

But her tactics were not merely hidebound to a set of formulas; she remained alert to exploit any advantage or weakness in the enemy dispositions that presented itself. Nor did she so involve herself in skirmishes and maneuvers that she lost sight of the strategic objectives of the war. She knew about the convoy of rusty and patchwork vehicles abandoned near the shore, the convoy that had transported the supplies and equipment of the entire Rathug army. Much of that materiel had survived intact, and could be invaluable in the forthcoming battle.

But the annihilation of the Rathugs and their auxiliaries had been so complete that none of the drivers had survived. Nobody in her own army knew even how to get the vehicles started, let alone drive them. That there might still be more drivers somewhere on the island was first suggested to her when one of the last Rathug outposts—perhaps forewarned of her mass-assault tactics—managed to escape in three trucks before she could come up with her army.

She sought information about drivers the moment that she made contact with Derek's forces.

It turned out that a number of men here had once driven trucks for the Brotherhood of Diablo. She sent one truck filled with former drivers down to the coast; by mid-afternoon she got back a whole convoy of trucks loaded with cannon and barrels of powder. And Gunnar.

He started bombarding the eastern ramparts at once. The few cannons still inside the sprawling fortress were quickly moved to face him—and even more quickly blown from the walls. Meanwhile the trucks returned to the coast for the rest of the ordnance salvaged from Colinga Harbor. By late afternoon the barrage was tremendous.

Eva had already organized the combined forces into an effective army. There were hundreds of escaped slaves now straggling in from all directions, and every one spoke the name Derek the Hunter with awe. But most of them were in such wretched condition that all Eva could do with them was to see that they were properly fed.

"Anything new to report?" she asked Jana.

"Those cannons are giving me a headache, and I'm getting sick from smelling those nasty trucks." She winced and held her fingers in her ears. "It's very hard to concentrate."

"But Derek and your friend Willie are still alive?"

"Yes, but for some reason they've just started moving in opposite directions. I'm close enough to Willie, but I still can't talk to him. He must be underground somewhere." She frowned and shook her head. "Very strange things are happening."

"What do you mean?"

"Well, right in the middle of the Rath of Diablo there seems to be some very weird creatures. It's such a big smear of people that it's all hard to sort out. But there's one creature there that I can find easier than anybody but Willie. It's not a Rathug or one of those giants we caught in the pits.'' She shook her head. ''I really don't know what it is.''

''And that's what's so strange?''

''That and the invisible Rathugs.''

''Invisible Rathugs?'' Eva looked at her in alarm.

''Well, they're down there on the plain, moving in very straight lines from the north wall out to those big hills about a mile away. Do you see any Rathugs? I can't.''

Eva shook her head. ''All I see are our own troops massed along the northern wall. How could anything get through them unseen? Where's Margo?''

''Right over there, sitting on her throne like she was just crowned Queen of the World. I don't like the way she's got everybody bowing down to her, Eva. Look at that spooky way she's got her face painted. I'm sure she's up to something.''

''She usually is. But right now let's see if she has any ideas about these invisible Rathugs. Can you still find Derek and Willie?'' she asked, as they climbed the hill to where Margo sat overlooking the battlefield, surrounded by her worshipful entourage.

She nodded condescendingly as Jana explained the problem; then turned and clapped her hands three times. She whispered instructions to her chief lackeys and sent them scurrying down the hill. They filled several of the trucks with men and drove off toward the northern hills.

''What does it all mean?'' asked Eva.

''It means the expiration of the Brotherhood of

Diablo,'' Margo replied arrogantly. ''I had anticipated just such a contingency, but without Jana's extraordinary perceptiveness—''

''Oh, don't start that stuff, Margo!'' Jana stamped her little foot impatiently. ''Derek and Willie are trapped inside the Rath of Diablo, and they might be killed or captured any minute now. Just tell us what it means. Save all your long words and gloating until later.''

Margo sniffed. ''I should have thought that it would be obvious to the most pedestrian intelligence. The remnants of the Brotherhood of Diablo are retreating to some place where they can regroup and prepare a counterattack at some indeterminate future date. Avolation now remains their only prudent course—''

''But they're invisible!'' cried Jana, more impatient than ever.

''Only from the surface. They are merely transferring their treasury down a subterranean gallery, from whose adit they undoubtedly expect to proceed unharassed to the coast. They still have sufficient shipping at their behest—''

''What a dummy I am!'' cried Jana. ''A tunnel! But we can't let them escape.''

''They won't,'' Margo said quietly. ''You may have noticed that our despicable antagonists began deserting the walls of yond grisly fastness immediately subsequent to the onset of Gunnar's bombardment. Patently they are withdrawing to their citadel, which, I am informed, is a sometime maximum-security prison that has aggrandized through generations of unchallenged presumption.'' She nodded grimly. ''Criminals were once executed here in a very suggestive manner.''

Eva said, ''Then they plan merely to let us overrun their walls and besiege an empty citadel. Jana, can you find . . .'' But she noticed that Jana was standing silently by herself, as if listening to something very far away. She did not disturb her.

''Oh, Eva!'' she cried at last. ''They've captured Derek. He attacked a Mog so Willie could get away, and they caught him, and now the Rathagon has got him where he gives his horror shows—''

''Horror shows?''

''Remember, I told you about those weird creatures? That's where they've taken Derek. I'm not sure what it's all about. Willie just reached some old tower that he thinks is going to fall down, and it's above ground, and so now we can talk. He's so excited that I can hardly understand him. There's nothing he can do to help Derek by himself.''

''But he can help us,'' said Eva. ''How did he and Derek get into the fortress unnoticed? Ask him about that, and about the number of defenders still on the walls.'' Then she beckoned to one of the signal-girls and gave her a message.

While the bright-colored flags began to wave all over the battlefield below, relaying the message, Eva conferred with Margo. At last Jana came over to them and delivered her report.

"It looks to Willie like only the most important Rathugs are withdrawing to the citadel. There are still a lot of them scattered along the walls. They just drove off the last of the galley slaves that Willie and Derek liberated, but not before most of their cannons were wrecked. I thought those we saw drop from the walls had just fallen, but Willie says—"

"What does he say about getting into the fortress unseen?"

"Oh, that's easy. It's a collapsed tower—that must be it over there along the north wall—and Willie is coming to meet us with Buck and a girl named Tereza, who helped them escape." She cried, "Oh, look, here comes Gunnar!"

"Thought that's what it was about," he said, when Eva had explained her plan to him. "Let's go, small stuff." He set Jana on his shoulder. "I'll pick the volunteers on the way."

"So this pitiful stripling is Derek the Hunter." The Rathagon's eyes narrowed with malice. "I'm almost tempted to bring it with me, so that adequate time may be devoted to its torment and death. All it's good for now is a few minutes of entertainment before I leave."

The Rathagon looked at the moment like anything but a defeated ruler: an enormous, bloated creature with eyes of such malevolent cunning that they seemed to burn right through anything they fell upon, he sat on a carven throne encrusted with jewels. His bodyguard of Mogs hovered around him like the pillars of a ruined temple.

These were his private chambers at the top of the citadel, but there were no windows for assassins to climb through, and no approach to the Rathagon himself except under escort by two Mogs, each holding an arm. Derek lay sprawled near the foot of the throne—but not so near that he could ever reach it without being seized by a Mog.

The chambers were crammed with the treasures of a long vanished world. Obscene paintings and sculptures were everywhere; gold, silver, and precious jewels covered even the most mundane objects; gaudy curtains of silk, embroidered with crude pornography, hung from every wall. The carpets were of an oriental richness and color; the perfumed oil of the lamps mingled with incense, disguising the smell of the Mogs. It was a pirate's fantasy of splendor and opulence.

But the fantasy was now in disarray. Files of slaves hauled chest after chest of treasure into the chambers—the hoard of generations of rapine and pillage. Hulking Rathugs then took the chests and hauled them into an alcove behind the throne and down a stairway which opened through a disguised panel. The slaves who had brought the treasure here were not allowed to see where it went.

Nineteen of the galley slaves had been recaptured; they too disappeared down the hidden stairway.

"Look on and despair, Derek the Hunter," sneered

the Rathagon. "This is but a mere fraction of my treasure. Five times what you see here has already been removed to safety. When night comes I shall give the Rath of Diablo to your verminous rabble—for a while. By then I shall be far away, with all my treasure and my most loyal captains and warriors. In my own time I shall return here to punish those who have presumed to annoy me. I regret that your own punishment will last only until nightfall, Derek the Hunter." His eyes burned malevolently down through the folds of flesh surrounding them. "My beloved Soswa himself shall provide me with this last entertainment. His only fault is his impatience to enjoy himself."

There was a crowd of about thirty sleek spies and Judases to one side of the Rathagon's throne, the only slaves permitted to see the hidden stairway. When the last of the treasure had been brought into the chambers the citadel was sealed off from the rest of the fortress. The spies and Judases were the only slaves allowed to remain inside.

"You have done well, my faithful servants," the Rathagon addressed them, his eyes glittering with cruel mockery. "But there is still one last service that you must now render the Brotherhood of Diablo."

Ignoring Derek as if he really were mere vermin, he then rose heavily to his feet and waddled back into the alcove behind his throne; his bodyguard of Mogs surrounded him as he disappeared down the hidden stairway.

The last of the treasure had now been carried below. Only a few Rathugs stayed behind with the spies and Judases; they spoke softly among themselves, or strolled restlessly back and forth. A single Mog stood guard over Derek. The rumble of cannons was much louder up here.

At last a squad of Rathugs emerged from below; they carried armloads of stout poles and coils of rope. It seemed to amuse them to watch the spies and Judases obsequiously lay these out on the floor in neat ranks.

Nor could Derek imagine at first what was happening. Then the truth struck him, and he turned his head away in loathing and disgust. He had been afraid when they first dragged him up here, taunting and cuffing him every step of the way. But he was now resigned to death. All he hoped for was the chance to strike one final blow against the Brotherhood of Diablo before he died.

The poles and coils of rope had now all been laid out, although the spies and Judases still seemed perplexed about how these were to be used. A few Rathugs laughed sardonically at their bewilderment.

Then one of them gasped; then another; then all thirty were shrieking and jibbering in terror. They were the sleekest and best fed of all the slaves. They now understood what their last service to the Brotherhood of Diablo was to be. One by one they were clubbed and bound to the poles.

Then the Mog wrenched Derek to his feet; it towered over three feet above him, and its grip could have crushed his arm to the bone. It dragged him toward the hidden stairway as the last of the bound slaves were carried below.

An animal mustiness met him on the threshold. He could not identify the creatures emitting it, although he was sure that they were not human. At least, not completely human. The panel closed behind him with a dull thud.

"Stand still, Buck!" cried Willie. "Please! Just for a minute!"

He stood on tiptoes on Buck's back, trying to peek through a slit in the outer wall. The girl watched him impatiently.

"But why do you look out this way? Further, how can you know that your friends are coming at all? We receive no word. Do you look for them now?"

"No, I'm looking for Rathugs. I know where my friends are. They'll be at the collapsed tower in about twenty minutes." He jumped down from Buck's back and shook his head. "I don't get it. Rathugs are moving up and down in a perfectly straight line outside this wall, but I can't see them. It's like they're invisible."

She tried to control her exasperation; it was impossible to be really angry with the affectionate little creature. Besides, even Derek the Hunter had trusted his lucky guesses, and because of them they themselves had managed to evade the Rathugs for over an hour now.

"But why do we stay here?"

"No Rathugs anywhere around. We don't want to reach the tower until the last minute. My friends will probably be seen entering it, and the Rathugs—"

"They chase the galley slaves now, my little friend. Or fight on the walls. Those that don't all run to the citadel. And if we stay here . . ." She shook her head impatiently. "But you don't even listen to me now."

Willie remained silent for some moments. "Oh, Tereza! They're taking Derek down to that awful place below the Rathagon's chambers. They're all moving downwards now, even the Mogs."

She looked at him as at a fanciful child. "If you say that Derek the Hunter is still alive, then I must believe you. Yes, it must be true. Not even that filth of a Rathagon could kill him. But come now, my little friend. Climb upon your great dog-thing and let us go to the collapsed tower. It is now the last minute of which you speak."

There were a few Rathugs on the walls above, but the collapsed tower itself was unguarded. They reached it within ten minutes. The roar of cannons outside the eastern walls had not abated.

"How many you think come?" whispered the girl.

"Well, there's Jana, who's little like me. And Eva, and Gunnar, who Jana says is very good to have on your side in a fight, and five other men who came from beyond the mountains with Derek. Let's see, that's eight in all."

"Who is this Eva?" asked the girl suspiciously.

"I know her," said Willie. "She was captured by the Brotherhood of Diablo, but escaped. They thought she was a great prize because she's so beautiful. She's the woman of Derek the Hunter."

He sensed the girl stiffen, and he looked up at her. But she was staring right past him with a strange look in her eyes. Then they heard scrambling noises above them.

One after the other the men jumped down from the ledge, then Eva. Gunnar brought up the rear, landing heavily with Jana in his arms. He set her down and started to brush himself off—but then gaped in astonishment.

"There's two of 'em!"

Jana and Willie, looking like twin sisters (or twin brothers), stood hand in hand, chatting merrily as if they had known each other all their lives. Jana was showing off her bandaged hand. But Gunnar did not have time to be astonished very long—there was Buck to contend with.

Eva was trying to calm the great beast, whose excited prancing put everybody in danger of having his brains dashed out against the concrete walls or floor. Gunnar braced himself, as two huge paws draped themselves across his shoulders and a gritty wet tongue slurped him across the face. He was glad that he had a thick beard.

At last Eva got Buck settled down, although the twitching of his tail and an occasional happy whine showed that he was ready to go through it all again at any sign of encouragement. Then Eva questioned Willie very closely about Derek's capture, and he filled in the details that he had already transmitted to her through Jana.

"There's only the one entrance," he added. "All the windows were covered with bricks a long time ago. They always put my cage in a corner of the chambers where they thought I couldn't see what they were doing. But whenever the Rathagon gave one of his horror shows . . ." He suddenly looked distressed. "Oh, Eva, that's where they took Derek."

"And that's where we're going—now. Do you know the way?"

"Kind of, but Tereza here knows it much better. We wouldn't have been able to liberate the slaves without her."

The girl stepped out of the shadows, looking sullen and defiant. She knew that she was still wearing Derek's leather shirt, and that Eva had suspected as much. She also knew that this was the woman of Derek the Hunter, a woman more beautiful than any she had ever seen before. She felt like a mere child beside her.

"Will you lead the way, Tereza?" asked Eva.

A series of confused emotions passed over the girl's face, but she seemed unable to find anything to say. At last she merely nodded and led them hurriedly from the collapsed tower.

Buck now had to carry a double load, but he hardly noticed the increased weight. Gunnar rounded up any fugitive galley slaves that they came across, while Jana and Willie made sure that they didn't come across any fugitive Rathugs. All the Mogs were now concentrated somewhere beneath the citadel.

Chapter 17: Soswa

Derek was cuffed viciously from behind whenever he dared turn away from the horrors in the brightly lighted arena below him. But he could not keep his eyes from drifting toward the row of cages in the dimness just beyond. He could not quite discern the shadowy forms moving restlessly back and forth inside the cages. Some of them appeared vaguely human.

He himself was in a kind of cage. The room was about fifty feet square, sloping upward toward the hidden stairway from the top of the arena wall. Thick metal bars kept anything from reaching the spectators inside, although it was evident that these gruesome spectacles were usually witnessed by many times the number now present.

The Rathagon, still surrounded by his bodyguard

of Mogs, sat on an ornate cushioned chair only ten feet away. Nearby sat his entourage of Rathug captains, and a troupe of obese young women dressed with barbaric gaudiness. They all seemed to be enjoying the spectacle.

A naked man stood with his back to the arena wall. The four huge rat-things crouching around him were like the slimy creature that Buck had killed in the midden. They had been let into the arena one at a time, and with each increase in their number they had grown bolder. They were still wary of attacking anything as large as a man, especially in such bright light; yet their beady red eyes glittered watchfully, and they crept closer and closer.

Then a fifth rat-thing scuttled down the caged ramp into the arena, and a cynical cheer arose from the Rathugs and the obese young women.

But the cheering ceased when they realized that the man in the arena was not cowering and abjectly pleading for his life. No Rathug present had ever witnessed a slave face death with such resolution before. Even the rat-things seemed intimidated by his courage, although none weighed less than twenty pounds, and all had been kept hungry.

Sharpened steel claws, pointing downward from the top of the arena wall, kept anything from climbing out. The last of the recaptured galley slaves were lined up just behind them. Too few in number to be useful as rowers, they also had been condemned to provide one last service for the Brotherhood of

Diablo—a last entertainment before nightfall. The doomed man in the arena knew that they were watching him; more important he knew that he was now under the eyes of Derek the Hunter.

Then the rat-things attacked in a snarling, hissing pack. The man fought back courageously—kicking, punching, clawing—until he stunned one of the pack by hurling it against the wall. Once more the remaining four rat-things hung back warily, their beady red eyes hungry and watchful. The man turned and saluted Derek the Hunter.

Angry shouts arose all around Derek inside the barred room. He, too, wanted to make a last gesture of defiance, but the Rathagon was still surrounded by his bodyguard of Mogs, unassailable by anything less than an army, a large army. Derek could only bide his time—and watch.

But the Rathagon himself had now watched long enough. He made an impatient gesture, and a moment later a whole pack of squealing, snarling, hissing rat-things came pouring hungrily down the caged ramp into the arena. Once more the Rathugs cheered, but still the doomed man would not cower or plead for his life. Flailing and pummeling with all his remaining strength, he was literally torn to pieces before he was at last dragged down.

Then the Rathagon made another impatient gesture, and two more galley slaves were hurled bodily from the wall. They had dared to cheer the courage of their doomed comrade.

But they too were resolved to die like men. Although one injured his ankle on landing, he was up at once; both slaves charged resolutely into the midst of the hideous pack of rat-things, actually driving them back. They too saluted Derek the Hunter, fighting courageously until they were at last overwhelmed and torn to pieces. Never had slaves shown such courage and defiance.

The Rathagon sneered, "So these vermin would impress this pitiful stripling. Let's see how much courage he has of his own. Show him the cages!"

Two Rathugs with torches entered the dimness beyond the arena. As they moved down the row of cages their torchlight revealed a collection of nightmare creatures: beast-things that had tried to be human, humans that had tried to be beast-things, creatures that looked like nothing else on earth. There were twenty-three cages in all, and no two monstrosities were even remotely alike.

"I've spent many years collecting them," said the Rathagon. "But they have repaid my efforts many times over, for each kills in a different way. Of all the things I have chosen to leave behind, I shall miss them the most." He laughed contemptuously. "How do you like my pets, Derek the Hunter? Or perhaps they're still too far away for you to appreciate? Don't let that disturb you. I promise to soon bring you much closer."

The brutal laughter of the Rathugs rang through the barred room. But Derek only returned the malevolent glare of the Rathagon with loathing and contempt. There was a snarl behind him and he was knocked brutally to the stone floor.

"Contain your anger!" cried the Rathagon. "I won't let him die so easily as that. It is still two hours until nightfall. . . ." Then he noticed one of his captains trotting toward the barred room.

The underground enclosure was actually several times the size of the arena itself, which only stood in one corner near the sole entrance from the citadel above. Derek had already noticed that the chests of treasure and the slaves destined to provide food had all disappeared behind a cluster of dark pillars and abutments at the far side of the enclosure. An escape tunnel?

He had also noticed Rathugs with lanterns posted beside what looked like air vents in the outer walls—perhaps the only means of communication still open to the outside of the citadel. The Rathug captain trotting across the enclosure looked like he had just been passed some very important news indeed.

He stopped about ten feet from the Rathagon, and two Mogs moved forward and took him by the arms. Only then was he allowed to come any closer. Derek tried to hear the news, but it was whispered, and the Rathagon's cushioned chair was too far away.

He suspected that much of the Brotherhood of Diablo was being sacrificed to hold the walls until the Rathagon and his chief captains and warriors—the cadre of a new dominion—could escape to the coast. Were the defenses crumbling sooner than expected? How much damage was still being done by the freed galley slaves? If he could not hear the message, he could at least see the Rathagon's face. It suddenly went slack.

Then a racket in the arena below attracted his attention. A line of Rathugs moved steadily across the sand, beating their swords against their shields. The rat-things were driven back up the caged ramp and out of the arena. Then iron hooks were latched onto the protruding bones of the corpses and they were dragged out.

"I have now chosen to leave before nightfall," announced the Rathagon, sweat beginning to bead across his bloated face. "We are impregnable here, so we need not hurry. There is still time for a last entertainment—the best of all. Bring on Soswa!" Shouts of approval rang all about him. "I shall soon return here, stronger than ever, and many years shall pass before I have slaked my vengeance on the vermin who now annoy me."

A tremendous roar went up, and Derek was afraid in his heart that what the Rathagon said was true. Surprise and their own arrogance—the arrogance arising from generations of unchallenged dominion—had lost this first battle for the Brotherhood of Diablo. He himself would never know who won the last battle, or even who fought it.

The thought of Eva came to him like a stab of pain. He had come to know and appreciate her for what she really was only a short time before the events of war had torn them apart. She had always feared giving birth to a marked child while they lived together at Saluston. Would they have had children now—fine, healthy, beautiful children who would live in a world of freedom and peace?

Then he became aware that the caged ramp was now being rolled along its tracks at the top of the arena wall. It was fastened down in front of a cage with unusually heavy bars. All Derek could make out through the dim light was a huge whitish shape; unlike the other restless creatures it sat ominously still.

"Control your impatience, Derek the Hunter," said the Rathagon sarcastically. "You will meet the favorite of all my pets soon enough. We are impregnable here," he repeated, as if trying to convince himself. "There is no hurry. But before I introduce you to my favorite pet, Derek the Hunter, you shall first witness the scope of his powers. I want others"—he glanced back at the troupe of obese young women—"to witness the scope of my discipline. Clear the wall!"

The last of the recaptured galley slaves were mercilessly clubbed down. Then the women were led obediently out of the barred room and lined up along the top of the arena wall. Their barbaric gaudiness shone even more garishly in the bright lights. There were seventeen of them, and Derek had never in his life seen women so obese or depraved looking. They seemed to anticipate the forthcoming spectacle with delight. Perhaps because they themselves were not down in the arena.

At a sign from the Rathagon a heavy metal door in the arena wall ground slowly open, and another obese young woman was shoved naked out into the light. She looked bewildered at first, but when the door slammed shut behind her she screamed with fright. She called to those above her by name, but they only laughed sardonically. Then one of the other women made an obscene remark, and even the Rathagon himself joined in the sadistic laughter.

"A plaything of my warriors, Derek the Hunter," he said. "But a plaything who has displeased some of them. Her punishment will make the others more pleasant companions." His eyes had lost none of their malevolent cunning, but Derek noticed them glance every few moments toward the Rathug captain waiting for news at the air vent. "Watch how my pet toys with her, Derek the Hunter. And while you enjoy the sport, think how it will be when it is your turn."

The cage door slid open and the huge whitish shape very slowly climbed down. It reminded Derek of the illustration of the ape in the Edgar Allen Poe story "The Murders in the Rue Morgue"—except that it was much larger and more powerful, and its whitish hair was long and silky. There was a look of evil cunning on its face as it moved very slowly down the ramp. It seemed to be enjoying its victim's terror.

The woman screamed and screamed again, waddling heavily back and forth in her terror, calling pathetically to those on the wall above. But they only laughed at her. Perhaps they felt that any show of sympathy might land themselves down in the arena too. Perhaps they were just so depraved that they felt nothing at all. Some of the women even made taunting remarks.

The ponderous, evil-faced creature at last crept into the light. All its movements were slothlike; it creeped so slowly across the sand that the obese young woman had no trouble keeping away from it. But slowly, patiently, it herded her into the corner between the caged ramp and the wall. There were shouts and laughter all over the barred room, as if in anticipation of what was to come.

Derek did not understand what was happening. Despite her obesity, the woman should easily be able to evade her huge, sloth-like pursuer.

In fact, just as its monstrous paw was reaching out very slowly to clutch her leg, she dodged past it and pounded across the sand. The slothlike creature would never catch her at this rate. But just as she reached the center of the arena a strange thing happened. She continued to run—and got nowhere. A brutal cheer came from the Rathugs.

"Watch how my pet enjoys himself, Derek the Hunter," said the Rathagon—although he himself seemed mostly to be watching the captain listening for news at the air vent. Nor did he seem to be enjoying himself very much; sweat poured down his bloated face. "Good Soswa. I would give half my treasure to be able to take him with me. But not even my faithful bodyguards can master him when he is excited. Yes, watch him carefully, Derek the Hunter. Imagine how it will be when my good Soswa enjoys himself with you."

Terror was in the woman's eyes; her fleshy body strained impotently with the effort to escape; her mouth writhed mutely with the effort to scream. As in a nightmare, she knew that the monster was drawing closer and closer, and yet she could not seem to get away. She continued her running movements, but very slowly, so very slowly that the huge monstrosity was gradually overtaking her.

It could now reach her with its paw, but instead it circled slowly around her, seeming to relish her helplessness and terror. There were more taunts from the women above; the Rathugs laughed sardonically; even the Mogs seemed to enjoy the spectacle in some primitive way. At last the monster slowly reached out and broke one of the woman's legs.

She fell heavily to the sand. Suddenly she began to scream and writhe in pain, as if the monster had released her from whatever mental grip it had had on her. But she could no longer run away. The evil-faced creature squatted beside her, and with hideously slow movements began tearing gobbets of flesh from her body, careful not to rend her in any vital place. It seemed to understand and relish the applause of the spectators, and did not want the spectacle to end too soon.

Derek realized that several of the Rathugs were watching his own reaction; he also realized that the Rathug captain was again hurrying across the enclosure with some further news. Its effect was startling. The Rathagon leapt to his feet and began screaming commands. Then the whole enclosure was in turmoil.

The obese young women were pulled from the top of the wall and hurried toward the escape tunnel. The Rathagon hurried from the barred room, surrounded by his bodyguard of Mogs. The entire contingent of Rathugs tumbled from the tiers of benches and hurried after them. Derek was dragged roughly to his feet and shoved out into the enclosure. The Rathagon stood shouting down from the arena wall:

"Good Soswa, put that one aside. I have another for you. This one will be more fun. Put that one aside, Soswa. Good Soswa!"

The creature looked up at him with its blood-slavered maw; there was an evil cunning in its eyes, and it seemed to understand. The woman was still alive and conscious, and it dragged her across the sand and laid her just inside the ramp, whence it could later carry her back to its cage. Then it emerged once more into the light.

"I have chosen to leave now, Derek the Hunter," the Rathagon blustered. "When I return to exact my vengeance, I shall be stronger than ever, and will see to it that the invincible Brotherhood of Diablo is never again challenged. But by then you yourself will be mere dust and gnawed bones.'' He cried, ''Here's a new toy for you, Soswa.'' And Derek was hurled from the wall.

He landed on his feet, stumbled forward, then regained his balance without falling. He glanced quickly up at the walls, but they were already deserted. Whatever news the Rathagon had just received, it was obviously very urgent. He turned to face the monster.

It sat at the mouth of the ramp, as if appraising him. Then all at oncc a strange feeling came over him: a vague desire to just surrender, as if he did not really want to escape. His will to resist was insidiously being leeched away, and he understood how so slothlike a creature was able to capture its prey. He also understood that it was still only toying with him, that its full powers of control would be far stronger. Very slowly it began to move toward him.

He glanced up at the sharpened steel claws encircling the arena; surmounting them would take an extraordinary feat of agility. It would take a mighty run and leap even to reach them. He considered trying to scramble over the caged ramp, but then he saw that it was studded all over with razor-sharp spikes.

He tested himself. All his limbs were still free to move although they felt vaguely stiff and feeble, as if he had just awakened in the morning. The desire even to try and move was growing weaker and weaker all the time.

The whitish monstrosity was now within ten feet of him. Derek hoped that it was as slow mentally as it was physically, for he needed a good run to build up enough speed even to leap up onto the steel claws. Without warning, he dodged past the monster and raced straight at the nearest wall. Then suddenly it was as if he were trying to run through water up to his neck. The creature's mental reactions were very quick indeed.

He remembered a dream that he had once had at Saluston about sinking into a tar road, and how he had to strain his whole body to move at all. It was like that now. But he did move—just barely fast enough to elude the leisurely grasp of the monster. It snarled and grimaced hideously. It sensed that it was being resisted.

Derek's pace was only that of a slow walk although he was straining to exhaustion all his great strength and speed. His whole body trembled with the effort; perspiration ran in streams. He felt he was trying to run with a hulking Rathug sitting on each shoulder. Stronger and stronger came the call to surrender, sapping his will to resist. His own movements were now equally slothlike, and he watched in horror as the huge paw began to reach very slowly for his leg.

Then suddenly he was dashing forward so fast that he barely kept himself from smashing into the arena wall. The creature's mental hold had somehow been broken. What had happened? He whirled around. But it no longer seemed interested in him. Snarling and grimacing, it looked in every direction for its invisible antagonist, then turned and lumbered slowly toward the wall directly under the barred room.

At that moment two little faces peeked down through the bars. The monster screamed at them in anger and frustration; its huge paws slowly clawed the air in its rage to grab them. But Jana and Willie only grinned impudently back at it, then began making faces and sticking out their tongues.

Derek was now out of the monster's range of vision, and he turned and raced headlong at the opposite wall. But just as he leaped for the steel claws above him, his whole body suddenly went numb; momentum alone carried him onto the very edge of the arena wall. For several moments he lay there as if paralyzed.

Then he heard another angry snarl in the arena below, and once more the creature's mental hold was snapped. He rolled over and looked up. Directly above him loomed the cages of the Rathagon's hideous pets. They moved restlessly back and forth, watching him with hungry eyes.

Chapter 18: A Want of Discipline

A snarling, screaming, howling uproar followed Derek as he worked his way down the row of cages; long shaggy arms groped for him through the bars, powerful forelegs tried to hook him with claws. As he at last reached the end of the deadly row he became aware of the turmoil erupting at the far side of the enclosure. Choking and coughing, a mob of Rathugs came staggering out from behind the cluster of dark pillars and abutments that screened the escape tunnel. Then a score of huge Mogs, and at last the Rathagon himself. Derek smelled smoke.

But he did not want to be cut off, and raced around the top of the arena wall toward the barred room. He reached it just ahead of the first Rathugs, leaped through the barred door, and slammed home the bolts. And there was Eva, and Gunnar, and Jana and Willie. Two big green lights came flying out of the darkness, and he braced himself.

But even Buck seemed to sense the urgency of their getting away before the Mogs arrived and began tearing out the bars protecting them. The smoke was getting thicker; the Rathugs and most of the obese young women had cleared the tunnel, and it looked like efforts were already being made to seal it off. The Rathagon and his bodyguard of Mogs were moving toward them.

"Just a few minutes more," cried Jana. "We're almost finished."

"Soswa's not really very bright," added Willie.

Then they both concentrated despite the mob of Rathugs bellowing and pounding futilely at the bars all around them. Soswa was also pounding at bars, the relatively thin bars of the caged ramp; his pounding was not at all futile.

"He's out!" cried Willie, clapping his hands. "Now for the fun!"

"The Rathugs don't think it's fun," said Jana, laughing merrily.

The pounding at the bars stopped abruptly the instant that the Rathugs became aware of Soswa moving slowly around the top of the arena wall toward them. The closest Rathug drew his sword and started to thrust—and suddenly was thrusting in slow motion. Soswa reached out very slowly and tore off his arm.

"No, Soswa!" cried the Rathagon. "Good Soswa! Go back!"

But the evil-faced monstrosity was too angry and excited to be stopped. None of the Rathugs in its way seemed to realize that it was really trying to get at Jana and Willie inside the barred room. Then the Mogs lumbered toward it. Despite his rage, Soswa hesitated—and so did the closest Mog. But the others kept coming.

"I told you he wasn't very bright!" cried Willie. "He can only control one mind at a time."

"He needs help," said Jana, and they both concentrated.

Soswa now turned and retreated slowly through the thickening smoke. But he was also able to slow the Mogs down, even though he could only stop them one at a time. He reached the row of cages and began tearing them open one by one. Unlike Soswa himself, most of the horrors inside moved very quickly indeed. The smoke and excitement had goaded them into a frenzy; they ran screaming and jibbering wildly out into the enclosure, attacking everything in sight.

The Mogs fell back to defend the Rathagon—all but one. It had nearly reached Soswa, and kept coming. But then it was suddenly rooted in its tracks. Soswa climbed the frozen giant like some colossal sloth, and very slowly began beating its face into jelly.

"This smoke is getting bad," cried Jana, rubbing her eyes

"That's probably Margo's work," said Eva, after

she and Derek had embraced. And she explained about the escape tunnel.

"Well, Margo didn't do it herself," said Jana. "She's right outside this place."

"Why don't we join her," Willie suggested. "And soon. I don't know what we're going to do when those Mogs break out of here. It looks like they've already smashed most of the Rathagon's pets."

"Except Soswa," said Jana. "But they'll probably get him too, pretty soon. He's too dumb to control them all at once."

"Here, Buck!" cried Derek. "Let's go, you two. We've got to get out of here fast. In fact, it looks like we'll have to withdraw all our forces for the night."

Eva agreed. "We may have a long siege in front of us."

"Maybe not," said Willie, as they climbed the hidden stairway back up to the Rathagon's chambers. "They haven't any water. Derek and I took care of that."

"But they have got Mogs," said Gunnar. "And an escape tunnel, where they can still dig their way out anywhere along the line. Let's get out of this place as fast as we can."

"By the way," said Derek, "how did you get in?"

"We were on the stairs behind you all the time," said Jana. "Willie knew all about the hidden stairway."

"They tried to hide it from me," he said. "But it was easy to figure out. We couldn't do anything, though, until the Mogs went away. By then they had put you down in the arena with Soswa."

"He couldn't even find us at first," said Jana. "He just slows people down so he can catch them. It was easy to get him mad. We could talk to him, but he was too dumb to talk to us."

"Look," cried Willie, "they're sealing off the entrance again, after our men worked so hard to get it open."

The metal door had been replaced on its hinges, and the wall around it hastily repaired. Derek and Eva looked at each other in wonder. Whose idea was this? It certainly wouldn't keep the Mogs inside very long. In the distance they heard the heavy chugging of engines.

Korso bowed stiffly. "Her Wisdom wishes to be informed the moment all our people are out of the citadel. Are there any more below?"

Derek looked curiously at him. "No, we're the last."

"Then please step out into the corridor." He signaled to his crew, who immediately resumed their work of resealing the entrance, every crack of which was painted over with thick tar. "To your posts!" he ordered a troop of messengers who were standing by.

The men saluted, clicked their heels, and raced off in both directions around the citadel. One after the other, engines began to chug at full throttle all around them.

"I don't like it," muttered Gunnar, as they descended the ramp. ''Probably don't even know why they're smearing that black stuff around the door. I certainly don't.'' He tugged fretfully at his beard. ''Just too many of 'em like that now, ready to take Margo's orders. I think that little smartypants is getting just too big for her breeches.''

Meanwhile Derek and Eva lagged behind the rest. They had much to talk about, strategy and tactics to discuss, and not much time in which to make their decisions. So long as the Rathagon could command so many Mogs and Rathugs the Brotherhood of Diablo was still powerful. They might still break out and escape.

''We can't keep our army in the field much longer,'' said Eva. ''We've already exhausted the powder and shot for our cannons, and we need supplies and reinforcements.'' She stopped and listened. ''What's the purpose of all those machines?''

''Let's find out. They seem to be just below us, all around the base of the citadel. I hope Margo hasn't got some scheme for digging through the walls. The Mogs will get out on their own soon enough.''

The first engine they came to was tended by four of Margo's personal entourage. It rested on blocks, with a long exhaust hose running upwards to an air vent, which was hermetically sealed with thick tar. There was a similar engine chugging noisily at each air vent that they passed. But they never did find Margo herself.

''She's on her way out of the fortress now,'' said

Jana. "And she's got a lot of people around her. Easy, Buck! It's only a machine. What's she up to now? Creating a big stink . . ." Suddenly she fell silent, her little head tilted slightly to one side. "Willie, they're vanishing!"

He nodded. "Maybe Soswa's tougher than we thought." And they both broke into merry laughter.

Then Jana explained: "There were hundreds of them inside the citadel when we left, but now there's less than half that many."

Willie added, "They seem to be going out like candles."

At last Derek understood the purpose of all the engines, the sealed doors and air vents. He had read about a cold-blooded system of executing criminals that had been used at certain prisons before the cataclysm. Margo's gas chamber was only on a larger scale.

"What does it all mean?" asked Gunnar.

"It means that we now have no more battles to fight against the Brotherhood of Diablo," replied Derek.

The battery of engines continued to chug at full throttle as they climbed the ramp toward the surface. It was twilight, and a rose-purple glow filled the sky.

"It's their endurance you g-got to watch for," Stinky observed, as he repeated the details of his heroic run for still another audience.

Derek's original encampment had grown since yesterday into a sprawling tent city, although it had lost none of its efficient organization due to increased size. Most initiative and responsibility had been left to the elected captains, and they had responded in kind. But the largest and most efficiently organized tent of all was that of the Wise Woman.

It was evening; since early this morning it had been known that the last of the Brotherhood of Diablo had perished, and many were still celebrating. But hundreds more had now gathered near the entrance of the Wise Woman's tent. They sensed that something important was about to happen.

Stinky continued, "They'll r-run all day at their own pace, if you let 'em." He added sagely, "So whenever a pack of dog-things c-comes after you, you got to run as h-hard as you can."

"That sounds reasonable," one man said dryly.

Then they all felt the tenseness, and the crowd of men and women fell silent—partly in awe at the approach of Derek the Hunter, partly in anticipation of the showdown that they knew was coming. Several mandates issued by the Wise Woman this morning had been overruled by both Derek and Eva.

Gunnar shambled along behind them as they strode through the parting crowd; the two little mascots skipped along at his side. Stinky left his admirers to join them.

Margo sat on a dais like a living idol, dressed in silken green robes, her face painted more exotically than ever. Spreading outward on either side of her throne, like the wings of a great bird of prey, were her obsequious followers—some inherited from the old Wise Woman, even more acquired by herself. The atmosphere was somewhere between a mysterious oriental fane and the totalitarian halls of a dictator. Margo watched them approach the dais with cold, calculating eyes.

"The Brotherhood of Diablo has been overthrown utterly," she cried in her shrill little voice. "In the establishment of our new suzerainty nothing must be left unchanged. All old cohabitations of significant extent must be razed and new ones constructed. All cohabitors must be transferred to new and unaccustomed provinces. No rank, possession, honor, or preferment must be allowed to proceed from any source but that of the suzerain. This is patently our wisest course, and yet I find that all my mandates have been abrogated."

"We have indeed won a great victory," Derek said patiently, but loud enough for all the hundreds of people crowded into the tent to hear. "But we now have a world to rebuild, and all those who contributed to our victory must be allowed to determine together the wisest policies. Even those who could make no contribution, who only suffered under the long tyranny of the Brotherhood of Diablo, will be heard. I have summoned a Council to meet next spring. They alone shall determine how the world should best be organized to ensure peace and freedom for all mankind."

There was a burst of applause, and even some of

Margo's obsequious followers began to look uncertain. Willie had to keep Jana from adding a few comments of her own.

Margo said coldly, "Economically as well as institutionally the world is in disarray. There is no cogent argument against the need for utmost efficiency in attaining its reorganization and compliance. Nor is disputation at all salutary where the most effectual procedures are well known. It behooves us only to devise an adequate system of coercion to insure their being effected. Put epigrammatically, the best interests of people are best determined by those best capable of determining them. We need discipline, not debate."

"That kind of discipline is only effective in the short run, Margo. Usually a very short run. The only really effective discipline is self-discipline, and coercion should only be resorted to reluctantly, and then as a very last resort."

Margo sniffed. "Things as they are, not as they should be, is the only secure foundation of any political calculation. To allow one's thinking to be clouded by specious humanitarianism is to give hostages to inefficiency. Intelligence alone must and shall determine both our future precepts and practice."

"Intelligence is indeed important in the ordering of human affairs. But character is at least as important, and it can only develop where people are free to choose and have at least some voice in governing their own affairs. Any people long deprived of both rights and responsibilities must inevitably become corrupt, and a corrupt people are incapable of either peace or freedom. Nor in the long run are they even very efficient."

"Precisely my contention," cried Margo. "No people inured to servitude, and necessarily ignorant of even the rudiments of self-government, can be trusted to order their own affairs wisely. You are now universally esteemed for great enterprises and prowess, and this allows you to abrogate my mandates in favor of those half measures which must inevitably lead to ruin."

"You cold-blooded stinker!" cried Jana, pulling away from Willie and shaking her tiny fist. "If I was just a little bigger I'd come up there right now—"

But Willie at last got his hand over her mouth and held her while she danced up and down in anger. There was laughter, but Margo also sensed that the opinion of those around her was turning more and more against her. She needed allies.

"You have not yet given your opinion, Gunnar," she said. "You are also universally esteemed for great enterprises and prowess. What is your opinion of our patent want of strong and immediate discipline?"

Gunnar rubbed his nose, tugged at his beard, and wiped his big paw across his forehead. "Well, first of all, it's my opinion that there's too many people around. This is kind of a family affair, and I think it would be best settled among ourselves."

Margo looked quizzically at him for a moment.

But she knew that her position was logically unassailable; therefore it followed that he was only concerned about seeming to disagree in public with Derek the Hunter. She clapped her hands three times, dismissing her entourage. The rest of the spectators reluctantly followed them out of the tent.

"Now, Your Wisdom," said Gunnar, "you come with me, and I'll give you my opinion about a want of discipline."

There was a curtain behind the dais, screening Margo's personal quarters, and Gunnar led her behind it. A moment later there was a muffled cry of surprise, followed by a series of rapid slapping sounds. At last Margo reappeared, rubbing her backside. Jana cut such merry capers at the sight of her that none of them could resist laughing. Gunnar followed Margo out into the tent with a stern look in his eye.

"Remember old Clara Johnson," said Eva in a consoling voice. "All her life she sought only more power, and it turned her into a warped and twisted thing. It is not the place of wisdom to seek power, but to guide it. Only when learning and power act together, each playing its own proper role, does the world progress. For whenever either of them acts alone, though they follow different paths, the result is always the same—tyranny. You are our hope for a better world, dear. Without you we could never have defeated the Brotherhood of Diablo, and we now need your wisdom more than ever."

Margo turned slowly from one to the other. Despite her exotic makeup, her robes of green silk, and her intelligence that couldn't be measured by any known test, she looked at the moment like nothing but the gaunt, lonely, nearsighted little girl that she really was. At last she nodded wryly.

"It seems that it's time I washed the paint off my face."

Jana stepped forward and affectionately took her by the hand.

Chapter 19: Epilogue

Winter passed and spring came once more into the world. New fields were sown; new herds of cattle were gathered into pastures all around the New Sea; the fleets of the Fisherfolk now plied the seas in safety. From islands, deserts, mountain refuges—from wherever people had fled the evil depredations of the Brotherhood of Diablo—the survivors of a decimated planet came forth again. Derek's messengers eventually reached them all.

The castle had once been a millionaire's toy; it now seated a Council of representatives sent from far and near, and they deliberated for many days before an agreement was finally reached. Derek and Eva were unanimously voted joint sovereignty; but the details of the new constitution took much longer to work out. The guidance of the Wise Woman saved them from many serious blunders.

Through firmness and patience Derek and Eva continued to hold her in check. While they strongly encouraged her organizational abilities, her brilliant plans for land development and food production, and especially her program for salvaging books and works of art, they discouraged her use of coercion to accomplish her will, and soothed her resentment at all forms of compromise. The final settlement was a solid foundation upon which to build a new world.

Nor was there to be any form of coercion in religious matters. Although both Derek and Eva had come to recognize that religion was ultimately the only secure foundation of any society, they determined that here too all peoples must be free to choose. Churches were already beginning to replace the humble tabernacles in which those who had escaped the Children of Satan had furtively taught the people. Now they also taught those who would someday become teachers themselves.

Prayers for guidance had preceded the sitting of the Council. Margo alone remained coldly aloof while they were being said; she evidently believed that her own guidance was more than sufficient.

Curtains covered the Professor's scientific apparatus, and his granddaughter Marie had arranged the great hall of the castle to look like one of the banquet scenes in her books of heroic fantasy. By her side stood the triumphant Stinky, at last elegantly dressed and bathed; his days of heroic running were now over, and he no longer needed all his strength. His adoring Marie listened with shining eyes as he told her once more about how he had outrun the pack of dog-things, which had already grown in size and ferocity.

Eva sat nearby, dressed in a loose flowing gown, for she was now with child. Derek stood attentively at her side, and they chatted with several representatives to the Council. Among these was the dark-eyed girl Tereza, who represented her mountain people far to the south. People were still arriving for the banquet, old friends and new.

Jana and Willie seemed to be having the most fun—and Gunnar the least. The two little people stood hand in hand at one side of the heroic fireplace, grinning mischievously. Gunnar stood miserably at the other with his wife. They had just been officially married in one of the new churches, which seemed to make her more possessive than ever.

"Here comes another one," Jana whispered.

Many of the signal-girls had been invited to the banquet; most of them had the long legs of the Wise Woman's people, and they all made a point of saluting their chief.

One girl strolled enticingly right up to Gunnar, hardly noticing the glares from his wife. Jana and Willie were too far away to overhear every word, but the girl's eyes never left Gunnar's, and there was no doubt what they were saying. At last she turned and strolled away, and there was no doubt what her hips were saying either. Gunnar tugged at his beard and wiped his big paw across his forehead; he seemed to look everywhere but at his wife.

Then a very old man entered the hall, and for once even Margo seemed happy to see somebody. Old Tom had taught her to read, and even found a candle-lighter for her so that she could read secretly at night in the storage space of her family's cell at Saluston. He had more than kept his promise of pulling his own weight. All of his friends from Saluston days, including Derek and Eva, came over to greet him. He had only just arrived from the logging camp.

"Just had the fright of my life," he said. "And that's saying something."

"Thought you were up in the library, old timer," said Gunnar. "What could be frightening about that?"

"The librarian," said the old man, chuckling. "I'm from these parts, you know. Or at least what used to be these parts. My pappy was a lumberjack—used to let me whet his axe sometimes—and that's what I always wanted to be as a kid. Never got my chance till these last few months, and now I get tired too fast. Anyways, we used to live in a small town up in the mountains, and I liked to read the westerns and adventure stories at the library. But Miss Johnson the librarian would come down on me like a rattlesnake: 'Thomas, you go wash those hands before you touch these books!' And she'd see that I did it too."

There were chuckles of anticipation around him, as if some of his audience had already guessed what was coming. Even Margo had a sly look in her eyes.

"Well," Old Tom continued, "I no sooner sat down with an adventure story I'd read as a kid, when I hear this eerie voice behind me: 'Thomas, let me see those hands!' My hair stood on end, what's left of it, and when I turned around there stood Miss Johnson. I almost keeled over right there." He joined in the general laughter.

"It may have been the identical volume that you perused as a boy, Tom," said Margo with unusual softness. "Old Clara Johnson salvaged much of her library after the cataclysm, and I've had it transported here."

"Old is right," he said. "I'll never see eighty again myself, but I never saw anybody that old before. And do you know what? That old devil actually sent me back down the hall to wash my hands a second time before she'd let me touch any of her books." Once more he joined in the laughter.

"But I saw another book I'd read, while I was browsing up there. Like you say, maybe it's even the same book." He confessed shyly, "Used to read poetry too, sometimes. On the sly, of course. If anybody caught you at it, then you'd have to fight. But I always remembered some words by a poet named Eliot: 'The end of all our exploring/ Will be to arrive where we started/ And know the place for the first time.' And it looks like that's where we are now, back at the place we started. Let's hope we know it better, and don't make so many mistakes this time around."

The Rath of Diablo was razed utterly, and the land divided into fields and pastures; within a few years its very location was a matter of debate. Colinga Harbor was recolonized by the Fisherfolk, and thrived along with the rest of Diablo, which became in time one of the most prosperous and cultured provinces of the realm—a realm that was continually expanding into new lands and territories. It became the seat of a famous university, a center for scientific research and exploration. Much of the old lore was preserved, and there were many strange new discoveries.

As nature gradually selected out those unfit to survive the post-cataclysmic environment, fewer and fewer unknown creatures were seen in the land. Most of the dead zones slowly returned to life; although some remained sterile for generations, and strange creatures continued to evolve in their vicinity.

The expedition that Derek led back to Saluston was a disappointment. He and Eva had had intentions of coaxing the survivors out into the sunlight, but there were no survivors. At least, none that they could discover—although Jana and Willie, who had both insisted on accompanying the expedition, said that they felt some strange presences deep under the mountain. Exactly what they were, nobody ever learned. But the Gunks themselves had been incapable of surviving without the very people that they had overthrown.

The expedition was a success in one unexpected way, however. Just before dawn one morning, Buck led back into camp a creature nearly as large as himself. She was skinny and dirty, and her coat was in poor condition; but she had the same huge green eyes that glowed in the dark, the same retractable talons as sharp as razors.

Jana and Willie were very cautious about approaching her, but with time and patience—and an occasional swat from Buck—she was at last tamed. She put on weight and her coat grew thick and shaggy, and soon both little people were riding forth on all Derek's expeditions into new lands.

One day neither Jana nor Willie would ride forth anymore. They mysteriously kept to themselves, like two little girls (or little boys) who had a very special secret. Only after much gentle coaxing did the Professor learn what it was.

"It looks like their species is going to survive after all," he announced to Derek and Eva. "It's all rather strange."

"Which is it, Professor?" asked Derek. "You know that we only refer to them as *he* or *she* as a matter of convenience. Which of them is pregnant?"

"That's what's so strange," said the Professor. "They both are."

Eva was especially sympathetic, for her own days of fear were now gone forever; she herself had already given birth to a strong, healthy, unmarked son—the first of many fine sons and daughters that she was to bear. But Jana and Willie continued to remain secretive.

Then one day they went off by themselves, and each gave birth within the same hour. They nursed their young in private, and it was several weeks before they would let even Derek or Eva look at them.

The babies were rather small, but seemed normal in every way except for their bright violet eyes and an uncanny awareness of what was happening around them. They lay side by side on a clean little pallet, constantly tended by their affectionate parents. And it was not many years before they too were riding forth on great shaggy dog-things with eyes that glowed in the dark.

Gunnar was now getting on in years. His wife at last prevailed on him to resign as chief of the signal corps, although his military duties still occasionally took him from home. But he vowed to remain faithful, a vow he kept ever after—unless he ran into temptation, which was not seldom. His reputation for strength and prowess, of various kinds, spread far and wide over the land.

But it was his eldest son Rollo who eventually became the great man of the family. In the years that followed he was appointed Commander of the Fleet, and he led his ships into many distant lands, until his voyages and exploits became the stuff of legend. The name Rollo Sevenfingers was renowned through all the rediscovered world, and yet he never tired of sailing forth in search of new adventure. Although some cynical people claimed that his great wanderlust only arose after his marriage to the Wise Woman.

No single lifetime could span the regeneration of a ruined planet, nor even reach much beyond its own limited realm. Tyranny and despair still reigned in many lands not far from the New Sea; Derek and Eva often had to lead their armies forth to battle. The war that overthrew the Children of Satan was especially long and bitter.

But their sons and daughters grew up about them to continue the long struggle when their own strength began to fail; sons who were men of valor, daughters of wisdom and beauty. And when at last their days were over, they were buried with all honor, to lie side by side forever in the earth that they had fought to make free.